NOLWENN LE BLEVENNEC is a journalist and writer. She is editor-in-chief at *L'Obs*, and lives in Paris. *As the Eagle Flies* is her first novel.

MADELEINE ROGERS is a translator from French and Italian and has worked in publishing since 2019. She studied Modern Languages at the University of Oxford and Translation Studies at UCL. She lives in London.

AS THE EAGLE FLIES

Nolwenn
Le Blevennec

Translated from the French
by Madeleine Rogers

PEIRENE

First published in 2023 by
Peirene Press Ltd
The Studio
10 Palace Yard Mews
Bath BA1 2NH

© Nolwenn Le Blevennec, 2021

First published in French as *La trajectoire de l'aigle* by Éditions
Gallimard. This edition published by arrangement with Agence
Catherine Nabokov and Linwood Messina Literary Agency.

This translation © Madeleine Rogers

The translation of this work was supported by a grant
from the CNL (Centre national du livre)

Design by Orlando Lloyd
Cover illustration by Camille Deschiens
Typeset by Tetragon, London
Printed by TJ Books Limited, Padstow, Cornwall

To my mother, Christine Béroff

IN THE AIR

My days were spent scurrying around like some busy little mammal. Back then my children were still young. After work I would run to them. I mean I would literally run, risking the danger – the one no one ever talks about – of my brain bashing against the inside of my skull. Coming home from reporting, I would be so eager to see them that I'd leave my bag on the train. The camera roll on my phone was full of pictures of them: a work of documentation on the level of a suburban American obsessed with the tidiness of his neighbour's lawn. I was holding on to no less than four videos of my eldest dancing to the Crocodile Song, and I was incapable of deleting a single one. I had tried. They were the same, but different. The only limit to my devotion was that I never cooked for them.

In the spring of 2016, my youngest son was a little over a year old when, one evening, I didn't come home as quickly as usual. I had stopped by a drinks party on the third floor of the excessively large building that housed the newsroom of the magazine where I worked, a low-ceilinged, open-plan space with black cables running across the floor. I'd been working there for a good two years but had never really noticed Joseph, the artistic director. I hadn't ever given him much thought, even though he was considered the prodigy of the team. Even though he had a signature style: he always wore a polo neck. I remember, that first time, we talked about Boulogne-sur-Mer. I have a soft spot for that town, up there on the north coast, because of its highly competitive downsides (weather, low elevation) and because it relies on the primary sector, which I find quaint. Like the port of Guilvinec in Brittany. It's quaint, the port of Guilvinec. So that's more or less what I said, and that it was undoubtedly better to go on holiday there than to the South. I added that the Mediterranean is nasty, that the sea is too calm there, that the water is scummy and yellow, that it stings your skin. That it's disgusting.

Basically, I was talking shit, and Joseph let me know it. It was brilliant, because everything I said infuriated him, and everything he added made me laugh. It was like we were playing a game of Jenga, and it was getting vertiginously high. My face felt like it was sizzling; sparks were falling into my plastic cup of red wine. The conversation lasted twenty minutes, and it was like something was gently squeezing my insides the whole time. I don't know if I had yet noticed his extensible bottom lip, the strange bit of skin on his forehead that you'd sometimes feel like playing with, or his tendency to rock backwards and forwards while talking. These are actually his defining qualities. What I did notice was that I liked him, that he was about my height and that his hair was thick and curly. I thought, *You could definitely hide a rubber in there.*

Three years later, I find myself no more than ten metres away from the location of that first encounter. 1 January 2019. I'm on call in the newsroom, and my partner for the day is a colleague who's giving me the urge to run away: he wishes me 'Happy New Year' every time we make eye contact. As for Joseph, he took off several months ago. At the moment, he's exhibiting in Budapest. You can see a few pictures from his new life as an artist on Instagram, and on a few sketchy websites if you're not scared of getting a virus. Which is the case for me. He's living his best life. While here I am, scrolling endlessly through Twitter, where the outrage *du jour* is a climate-sceptic TV clip. It's pathetic. I end up clicking on my email archive, which doesn't bode well at all. I reread our messages in silence. But on this, the first day of 2019, I realize that these exchanges don't upset me. That my throat hasn't tightened. That they no longer intoxicate me. Everyone told me that indifference would break through in the end. I see that the moment has come.

So there you go: this is the commonplace story of a short-lived romance in the offices of a failing magazine. The story of the discovery that willpower can be annihilated. Devoured. Of a traumatic separation at the height of union, and the devastating crash back down to earth. The day after the break-up, I burst into tears at the first note of the prelude to *La traviata* – it's a B – at a concert in Metz. All three acts then passed without me managing to pull myself together. It was noisy. Ridiculous, to be honest. And disturbing for my neighbour. At the point when Violetta breaks it off with Alfredo ('*Dite alla giovine*'), I was hyperventilating, my head between my knees. After the concert, which had been a present for my mother's seventieth birthday, I slept next to her in twin beds with mustard sheets in a dreary hotel room. All of which – much as I love my mother – added to the feeling that I'd fucked up my life.

On the train back to Paris, my mind was blank, my body was exhausted, and the top of my head was itching. My mother pretended not to notice anything because she's afraid that I'm going to end up dying alone. Every time a threat hovers over my love life, she freezes like a lizard. When Joseph, fresh from the hairdresser's, broke up with me by the Assemblée nationale, I felt like a drugged-up dog abandoned by the side of the road after crossing Spain in the back of a dealer's speeding car. The wave of depression, immense as it was, was interspersed with moments of lucidity: *The good news is, you're not a dog.* And also: *You have discovered his limits* (Joseph's). And finally: *Bury yourself in other activities for as long as you need to.*

*

As you might have guessed (because if it's not forbidden, there's nothing to get so worked up about, you're just going to the cinema), we're talking about an affair. In its most widespread and tragic form: adultery with a profound disagreement over the desirable outcome. Nothing to do with conservative or religious values here, but rather two psychic structures in conflict. From the very first minute, there was no point of agreement between Joseph and me on the definitions of love, happiness or risk. For him the relationship had a settled meaning, while for me it was mobile. He held his words in, while I spilled mine out. If you're not afraid of psychoanalysis, you could say that my ego was inflated: his went into retreat.

In the spring of 2016, when I first met him, I was thirty-three, although I didn't look it – my face is ten years behind my age (this is something that will surely turn against me one day: I'll wake up in the morning and my cheeks will be slack; already I smoothen out less quickly). But my body was in line with it. Half firm. As I'd had two children in four years, I was about eight kilos overweight. Chubby arms contrasting with a slender nose. Good skin. I was gradually regaining my previous shape. In no rush, because I only ever saw myself when I had my photo taken (never) and because I had no one to seduce. Other than by the father of my children, I hadn't been penetrated in seven years. Unless you count the forearms of several midwives trying to check the dilation of my cervix.

During the delivery, those midwives had had to step over a short man lying on the floor, playing chess on his phone. He was twenty years older than me, and I had been living faithfully beside him ever since we first met. In perfect harmony. For as long as I've known him, my partner, also a journalist, has proved himself unsurpassable. Firstly in the sense that, without having to do anything at all, he has twenty years on me. But also in the sense that I've always found him more original than anyone else. He's something of a ludicrous character whose sense of humour is based on games, silly voices and imitations – and never sarcasm. He's also an obsessive, the incessantly rolling ball of a roulette wheel, and is always coming up with alternatives to alternatives – but we'll talk more about that later.

When I met Igor, in the summer of 2009, I was twenty-six and he was forty-six. I had just left journalism school and a relationship with a Lebanese boy who had chiselled abs, a strong nose, hair that bounced when freshly washed, and enough brains to pass the civil-service entrance exams. Igor was less disciplined. And less slim, although I discovered at that point that I liked it that way. His fat belly, which I came to fetishize, had the consistency of a cushion filled with rice (and it pressed down on me when we fucked, like hundreds of sexual organs).

In bed, Igor feels like a brioche. He's a soft round mass and I surround him like water. But as soon as his clothes are on – and I always find this surprising – he becomes an old grey-haired Russian. He sticks his chin out when he's thinking. Sideways on, in these moments, he looks like a bulldog. Round glasses and dark-coloured sweaters suit him: they make him look like he could be a McGill history professor. Yet Igor is also something straight out of a pantomime; it sometimes occurs to him, for no apparent reason, to raise his arms and let out a piercing ululation, like North African women do in moments of celebration. He rides his bike through the streets of Paris, leaving crumpled receipts and the last strains of 'La Madelon' (with all the Rs rolled) trailing behind him. Everyone in our neighbourhood knows who he is, because of all this, and also because he stood as a leftist candidate in the 2014 local election.

*

Igor and I met on a Saturday evening in Saint-Ouen, on an editorial deadline. I was on a temporary contract at my first journalism job, a current-affairs and photojournalism magazine. That evening, in his Established Political Journalist's office, he suggested I should interview Ségolène Royal, had a very long and very loud phone conversation with Bernard-Henri Lévy (whom he called 'Bernard' throughout) and made me listen to Mozart and Salieri on his computer. The audio was shit. He skipped from one clip to the other. His hand tapped out the rhythm on his desk. Could I hear the huge difference in talent? It was all ridiculous, and endearing.

That first contact took place a week before the death of his wife, at the age of forty-four. When our relationship started to take off, a month later, Igor was still crying in front of the Activia yoghurts in the supermarket and driving around in his in-laws' old car. It was inside that car that he kissed me for the first time. I didn't say no, but I pressed my lips together tightly to show him I saw complications down that path. Not the best start. After I'd left, I sent him a message to tell him he shouldn't think I always kissed like that.

In our first weeks together, I watched him the way you'd watch someone about to jump through a ring of fire. He was exhilarated and I was curious. But as the months went by, I got used to his ways, his superhuman energy, and how he needed me in order to survive. After his wife's death, Igor was all over me like a rash. Every morning, in my tiny attic apartment, he'd bring me a croissant and a can of Minute Maid orange juice. He followed me while I was out reporting. He would call me all the time: 'I'm on my way.' An excessive presence. Counter-intuitively, I started to love him because he would call me every half-hour, and then one day he didn't for over three hours. I missed his restlessness (I live my life *adagietto*, rather slowly; I take after my grandmother, who used to say, 'I can't wait to go to bed tonight,' from the moment she woke up in the morning). When, ten years later, I reread the fluvial messages he used to send me, it makes me choke.

This strangeness, now, when I don't really know whether I'm the only one wanting/believing in/thinking about/ hoping for tomorrows and day-after-tomorrows and on and on after that, without knowing for that matter whether I'm just extrapolating a temporary need (for you, for you, and for you again, in every possible way, but temporary all the same) or if something inside me has really recognized that the essential is there.

But at the time – I'm astonished by who I was then – I stashed them all away, and in the spring of 2010, ten months after we first met, the river of words having dried up, I decided I wanted to live with him. To cling to the cyclone. My body made it easy for me: I slipped over on an icy pavement and exploded my left elbow. My arm had to be kept still for three weeks. Thanks to these circumstances, I sublet my little apartment and moved myself in with him. I piled up my painkillers on his nightstand and waited for him to bring me food. Our whisperings usually began in the total darkness of the early morning. Later in the year, at daybreak, at his mother's country house in Beauce (which has two flaws: you can hear the main road in the distance, and it's located in a hollow, which makes bike rides difficult), I woke up and said to him: 'So, are you ready to start again?' On the uncomfortable mattress, under the musty covers pulled up around his shoulders, his little eyes shone. He replied: 'That's what we're doing already.'

The difficulties of our relationship – his grief, the existence of his two grown-up children and the birth of our own two – took up all my energy for years. For a long time, I felt like some kind of thalassotherapy special offer for the bereaved. It took me a good two or three years to soothe my jealousy over the fact that I hadn't been chosen over his wife, but to take care of him in her absence (and even then, not really *chosen*: I just happened to be in the office next door wearing a short skirt). A further year or two to stop feeling the need to put her down in my head. And then years more to feel affection for her and, finally, to relate to her.

By the spring of 2016, I was there. Soothed, relating to her. I was happy to see the Facebook statuses that Igor would post on each anniversary of her death. I checked who was liking them with benign approval. I wondered how she had managed to put up with Igor's mess for so many years, his habit of getting everything out and never putting anything away. I approved of the presence of her ID photo in his wallet. I knew that, now it was broken, the watch that she'd given him was in the top drawer of his bedside table, which was dedicated to that kind of keepsake. I hoped (and also feared) that he would write a book about her one day. Obviously, I was afraid of turning forty-four. She'll be on my mind from the very first second of that day.

So, on the eve of the beginning of the Joseph era, everything was going fine. Our complicated little family was doing well. We had moved out of his family apartment, where, on the wall opposite the bed, a photo of her in a turquoise bathing suit had still taken pride of place (I wonder now how I could have lived in that bedroom and slept in that marital bed, even if Igor went on her side and I took his). I got on well with their two children, who themselves had now each moved into their own one-bed apartments. In our new place there were still some photos of her – but not in our bedroom – and the furniture she'd chosen on the cusp of her fortieth birthday: a cabinet, a sideboard, a table, some black cushions. It was fine by me. Every day I was brushing past her belongings and catching up to her in age. I worked. I mothered my boys. In the evenings, after putting them to bed, I'd smoke a cigarette on the balcony while dreaming of the day when they'd have their showers on their own. I couldn't wait to have myself to myself again. Igor and I made love once a week. It was a good rhythm. The age gap was a turn on. My body, eternally young.

*

After the drinks on the third floor and our excellent conversation about Boulogne-sur-Mer, Joseph was also smitten. Three days later, I bumped into him near the office while I was having a beer with an intern. We were standing outside on the pavement. He came and stood on my left. Just centimetres away from me. And this time, I noticed how he rocked back and forth (I know now that if he's not moving his legs, he's crossing his arms instead). When I left, he followed me without having any pretext. Then he waited with me for the blonde, curly-haired friend I was having dinner with. She arrived and parked her scooter on the square. He lingered. She walked towards us, curls poking out of her helmet. He was still waiting. He didn't leave my side until, awkward at how we were all standing there, she asked if he was coming with us.

A few days later, I asked him to lunch. I took him to a restaurant which has the dual appeal of always being empty and also serving fresh sushi. He didn't like raw fish, but he went along with it. I told him about my life with Igor and the children; I gave a darker version of the story so as not to put him off (we all do it, but that's the image that will always stay in Joseph's mind; the way we look at couples we're scheming to destroy reminds me of the way a three-year-old looks at another kid's sandcastle). On the way back from the restaurant, outside the office, Joseph asked me if I'd like to take part in his project of creating a space on the magazine's website dedicated to art. Joseph was annoyed that our magazine always seemed to do its best not to stand out. We undervalued architecture terribly, for example, even though there was a niche to be filled. 'Mm, yeah, it's true, you're right.' Before we got in the lift, he uttered these words that I still find moving now: 'Our magazine isn't going through a crisis; it's going through six.' Here was someone who could manipulate an arbitrary opinion into absolute fact.

It was one idea out of the hundreds he had for saving us: in 2016, nobody was interested in weekly news magazines any more. An awkward publication schedule; a pointless recapitulation of the news. The summer went by with a few email exchanges about the website project. Once the page, which I'd vaguely helped to put together, was uploaded, I wrote to him saying it would be a relief to stop flirting with each other (which is what I, especially, had been doing). That's how I called for us to put our desire into words. He replied that he'd quite like us to continue. I remember exactly where I was when I read those first words, announcing the action. I was on my way to pick up my son from nursery, a metre from the entrance. I performed a triple somersault (in my head). That evening I was a mother in high spirits. Laughing as I picked up grains of rice from between the parquet tiles like it was the most hilarious thing in the world.

After that exchange, it was me again who suggested a drink. One evening in September 2016, we sat down at a table outside a bar-tabac. We talked for some time about the magazine and its financial situation: this was the pretext conversation, a sign of our good manners and of our feelings. At the end of *War and Peace*, when Natasha and Pierre are finally together and talking about anything and everything, Tolstoy writes: 'Just as in a dream, when all is uncertain, unreasoning and contradictory, except the feeling that guides the dream, so in this intercourse, contrary to all laws of reason, the words themselves were not consecutive and clear, but only the feeling that prompted them.'

Then the bar closed its shutters and we went across the road, to a touristy brasserie that stays open all night. There, surrounded by beer-drinking foreigners, the conversation arrived at its true purpose. Joseph told me that the situation was really bothering him because, if we gave it free rein, it would end with us packing up moving boxes. He would end up wanting to live with me. Since he liked the shape of my nose and my way of expressing myself, he was already daydreaming about us living together in a big, light-filled apartment. I didn't know what to say: I could picture the apartment and the light, but I wasn't quite there. I was fine where I was. I wondered in particular why it was a problem that he could see things going so well. He said, 'It's a problem because I'm a huge coward.' That made me laugh. Since when do cowardly men announce it with a loudspeaker? Since Joseph. I understood later: his technique involves showing the worst of yourself at a point when the other person isn't yet susceptible to getting upset about it. You can then consider them to have been warned. Declare all future complaints null and void. Wash your hands of it. In short, what I had taken for flirtatiousness was in fact part of his modus operandi.

So, that evening, when I was taking nothing of what he was saying seriously, Joseph explained to me that we wouldn't kiss, because it was all too heavy for us to actually go through with it. I made wide eyes at him: 'Obviously we're going to kiss. Of course we will, because we want to.' Towards ten o'clock we were back in front of our darkened office building. I wished I could make the fluorescent yellow child seat, reminding me of my imminent betrayal, disappear from my electric bike. I kissed him. I have no memory of how it felt. But I still have the image of him walking towards the opening of the Métro. He wasn't whistling. His body was tense. He was dreading something.

A few days later, I scored a second drink. Joseph told me he couldn't really see what there was to add to our previous discussion, but he still crossed Paris to come and join me. I still thought he was being a ridiculous tease. I was coming from a meeting with a far-right militant who lives in the tower blocks of Chinatown. The guy's an antisemite, but he has a fast way of talking and a strong Burgundy accent that always cheers me up. So I was in a bright and optimistic mood. And, optimistically, I once more announced to Joseph that I wanted to kiss him. While he once more explained to me why it couldn't happen: 'I met my partner very young and I've poured everything into being with her.' (Here he made a gesture of pouring water on someone.) 'The way you're making me feel is unprecedented. What I'd really like to do is put you under a bell-jar and keep you on my desk.' So, the life of a cheese, then. At the top of the Métro steps, he said goodbye.

I walked down the passage of that station in south Paris, one of the rare few I wasn't familiar with, shrugging my shoulders several times in different ways. Well. I'd been tossed aside. Igor had got me used to taking first and thinking later. Joseph, on the other hand, wouldn't even dare to touch. Okay then. Waiting for the train, I thought about the marshmallow test. The experiment where they sit a nursery-age child alone in a room with a marshmallow in front of them. They're given a choice: they can gobble it up straight away, but if they resist and wait for the researcher to come back, they can have two. There are the children who manage to wait (and will do well in life), and there are the others. And then there's Joseph, aged four, who never even opens his mouth.

In the days following that first goodbye, I felt myself coming down. My face lost its points of symmetry and my body got so weak that, coming back from reporting in Rouen, I fainted on the train. Keeled right over. Joseph found out and it gave him food for thought: perhaps I wasn't so threatening after all, if I was the sort to swoon on the train like a Victorian lady? The week after, while we were catching up, I told him off for his sang-froid. He had the manner of a Russian spy. He smiled, we parted ways politely. An hour later, he wound up sending me a message that he *wanted to see me right away*. (*I want to see you right now*, *Alone*, *Come*: Joseph pushes the eroticism of these authoritative phrases to its limit.)

I accepted, and there, in the middle of September, a hundred metres from the entrance to the office, on the terrace of a crappy boulangerie, was sitting a person who had completely changed his mind. Joseph announced with a solemn air that he was on board with our having an affair. He'd spoken to a friend about it, and she'd convinced him. She'd told him: 'Have it.' I heard: 'Have her.' I was no longer the thalassotherapy special – now I was a midnight snack. I didn't ask any questions, because I was delighted and because Joseph was already asking me plenty, like: 'So, when are we going away together for the weekend?' But also – and we spent more than ten minutes on this one – 'How will we message each other safely?'

Here's what I was hiding from myself: it's obvious that my priority was to feel his body against mine, while his was to protect his principal relationship. I was porous to all possibilities. Transported as if my life were on the brink of beginning again. He was waterproof, like most things from Muji. Before it 'took root', to use his expression, he would run off home to have babies. He wasn't planning on anything else.

*

There was Joseph's refusal, right from the start, to give us a real chance. There was a mountain of feelings between us that wouldn't go away. And there were the three years lost to pondering this paradox. 2016–2019.

It took me three years to understand that we really can push aside the affection and desire that we feel for someone. That we can even believe we have very good reasons for doing so. I came to this understanding mainly from reading piles of psychoanalysis. The first revelation was reading Freud's *Beyond the Pleasure Principle*, which describes pleasure as an organic stability and the death drive as a force which maintains it by extinguishing internal arousal. An interior firehose, if you like. For Joseph, whom I'm not afraid to define as a slave to his drives (without knowing if this is really a thing), I went very quickly from being a life drive (sexual) to a death drive (life-draining). Or, to put it another way: I'd been ingested and then spat out. Freud calls the mechanisms of expulsion from the subject *Ausstoßung*. I like that word a lot. You'd think it meant 'highway code' in German.

It also took me three years to understand that nothing can undo a person's tendencies. Neither the degree of affection nor the degree of desire, and especially not my willpower – however strong. In *Justine* by Lawrence Durrell, the narrator praises relationships built on the *repose of the will*. Repose of the will! When all your mental energy is devoted to working out how to keep someone, that sounds so good.

*

Joseph's exhibition in Hungary is over. I found out reading a mixed review in *Libération*. He should be back in Paris, but I haven't had any contact with him. I have the irrational fear that if I speak to him again he'll devour me, that my mind will again be under his sway. These past few years, I've developed a sort of PTSD: if he says five things to me, each sentence has to then be relived and digested, which can take several hours. I have to differentiate each statement and balance out what I heard, what I inferred, and what I understood. I become a marshalling yard: every sentence enters my body without judgement and I examine it. The more there are, the more time I waste. I think I started doing that when I realized that he too was ruminating over every detail of our conversations.

Things between us are well and truly over, but this evening, in March 2019, I want to tell Igor that Joseph's artistic success is making me urgently reconsider my own hopes and dreams. The father of my children has just got back from his oldest friend's sixtieth birthday. He asks if I want to hear the latest gossip from his group of friends. I say yes, but he starts talking about a couple I'm not familiar with. I interrupt him:

25

'Forget it. I don't even know who you're talking about.'
Then:

'I just got into it with my mother.'

'Oh, really? I wouldn't have known. When I left, you were just eating salad.'

'We were doing both. I told her I wanted to take up video art again, but she acted like she hadn't heard me.'

'You want to go back to Corrèze to film more trees? Sorry, but I don't get the appeal.'

I don't make videos any more, not since becoming a mother. It became too difficult to carve out the time for it without feeling guilty. At my house, like everywhere else, the word 'maman' is used thoughtlessly and often several times in a row. The child's interjection every time he surfaces from his thoughts. 'Maman' signals the return to the world after an absorbing three-minute activity. *Me again. I want some water, a toy, a piece of paper, you to look at me.* The result: a daydream pushed through a meat slicer.

'No, not trees. I want to go to Ouessant for a few days. I feel like I'm stagnating while you and Joseph are blossoming. It's unbearable. My life is one-dimensional, while yours are multi-faceted.'

'What? What has Joseph got to do with this? You're going to leave me alone with the children because of him? You're joking, I hope?'

'Okay, okay… But, Igor, have you ever once asked me permission to go and do something?'

'No! But it drives me crazy that Joseph's the one to inspire you to start it up again. You've got bad taste. I should've punched that guy in the face.'

'...'

'If I give you a foot massage, will you drop this Ouessant thing?'

(I told Igor about Joseph. I'll save the dramatic circumstances of this confession for later.)

(I'm a great user of *Okay, okay...* in arguments.)

As for my mother, if she didn't hear me when I was talking about video art, it's because a lack of confidence runs in the women in my family. She finds my career progression admirable. 'I have no doubt that you're a good journalist.' Read: you mustn't tempt fate. She passed down her taste for classical music and literature to me, 'But making something from the heart, that's another thing entirely.' She's known that making videos is important to me since she caught me filming my dead grandfather's feet from down the hallway. But she always avoids the conversation. She's afraid that what I make won't be up to the standards we hold.

The day after the argument, Igor tells me he's sick of everything that's been going on with me since Joseph came into my life. Sick of my WhatsApp conversations with my work friends, of my psychoanalysis, of my interior life in general, of the art books I bring home in bundles. And now, this business of familial abandonment. To hell with my independence and my provocative behaviour (synonymous here, clearly). And, by the way, he hasn't forgiven me for cheating on him. He's thinking about leaving me if I carry on being so self-centred. The day after that, he demands that we rediscover the 'bees' in our respective stomachs. The butterflies, you mean? He replies, 'Yes, I want passion, jealousy and sex if you want me to put up with your hare-brained pseudo-artistic projects.' I wonder if we're going to have to sleep together every day for me to go to Ouessant. If that's how it is, maybe I can't be bothered.

*

It was in September 2016, after that conversation on the terrace of the boulangerie, that the passion ramped up. Joseph's partner wasn't around. She was away somewhere on an assignment. Joseph let go of all his inhibitions. He effectively became the incarnation of the word *drive*. He lifted the supposedly decorative bell-jar and stuffed his face like a crazed animal. I'm thinking, as I write this, of pigs' snouts snuffling in bone meal. Or maybe of moles... What do moles eat? Anyway, you would have said he was giving in to his desire to devour me – and that he was afraid of being devoured himself in return.

At the start, I tried to calm things down. For our first proper date, we chose the famous reclining chairs in the Jardin du Luxembourg. I found him so articulate and intelligent and spent those first few hours making sure he didn't realize that I was less so than him. A metre or so away, some children learning to play tennis were laughing at us and how feverish we were. But we didn't discuss the moving boxes any further, thanks to my efforts. I declared that our affair would have to stop dead as soon as he started to make baby plans with his girlfriend. I was the embodiment of wisdom and experience. The responsible mother who wasn't about to leave her home and family after five minutes. Joseph acquiesced. *Yes, yes*. But it was already too late. He wasn't experiencing life normally, but in fits and bursts. A week had been enough for him to impose his behaviour on me and bring me to a state of arousal close to madness.

He wanted to be a drone, to follow me through the streets of Paris. He sketched the lines of my face and caressed my hair as if he couldn't quite believe it. He had read all my articles, even the ones about the menopause. He sought me out on the internet, as if I lived there. He inhaled everything Google had to say about me. He wanted to join Anonymous, to hack my phone and search it thoroughly, to plunder it, but that would be immoral and, anyway, he didn't know how. He asked himself how my existence could have escaped him for so long. *Where were you?* He wrote my name out a hundred times in blue on a napkin. He wrote a song about kidnapping me. Refreshing my Facebook page brought tears to his eyes. And then, he wanted to fuck me all the time and to tell me so. To be inside me. To bite my neck. He wanted me on my back, drenched, penetrated, burning, sticky, covered by him, underneath him, for me to see and feel how hard I made him. He wanted to send me into spasms and watch my pussy swell. Crave him. Beg him. Or have no choice but to cede to him. He would ask me to come and pleasure him right away, right there in his office in front of everyone (too bad if they didn't like it, he didn't give a fuck any more). He would masturbate for three hours straight. Teetering on the edge of orgasm so as to be able to start again later. He exhausted himself. Sometimes I would go home with my trousers wet down to the knees. He would talk to me while we fucked. *Where do you want to take it, and how?* Then, *Where do you want me to come?* He would always ask me where I was and when I was going to get there. It was urgent. His dick was rock-hard and throbbing. Fuck, where was I?

He wasn't listening to the friend he was having dinner with because there was nothing but me, everywhere, behind his eyes. And for my part, I was just going to tell him that his eyes were more beautiful to me than anyone else's had ever been. To tell him, too, that I'd like to spend my whole life eating the German pastry that his surname made me think of. When it appeared in my inbox, I practically licked it, I turned it over and over in my head before resigning myself to making it disappear again by opening the message. I told him how good it was to wait for it. To be a minute away from reading it. In just one week, this was the extent of the damage.

In this rhythm, my body very quickly entered a state of general overstimulation. My head was invaded by explicit imagery. To give myself up to it all day long, I could have thrown all my loved ones into the sea. Sold my parents out to the police. Yelled insults down the office corridor to get myself fired without notice. Joseph's words circled around my head for hours. It took a long time for them to sink in because everything was immoderate and unrestrained. His perfect erotic emails made my core tighten. *I'd start by... Then all of a sudden I'd pull out, and that would make you sad.*

But in the heat of this language, my sense of pride couldn't nonchalantly stretch out like someone unwinding in a sauna. No, it was the first time anyone had spoken to me like this, and it was killing me. In that autumn of 2016, I was living beyond my means. In *Of the Farm*, John Updike writes that he was so happy in love, his heart seemed to trespass the limits set to joy. For me, it wasn't about joy. It was hitting me hard, and it was painful. It was like the needle of a metre tapping obstinately against the maximum. Oscillating beyond the red zone until it hurts. Incessantly, and so hard that it might be better, for it and everyone else, if it broke instead.

While a redundancy scheme was taking place at the magazine, while the latest bad news was being exchanged in the general meeting, while our industry was collapsing in corridors where young journalists cried, the two of us were breathing in each other's necks. *Come to the GM, I want to be close enough to smell your perfume.* We couldn't give a shit about target charts or the terminations of whoever had the fewest HR points. Our apolitical brains were awash with oxytocin and dopamine (source: *Marie Claire*). We would comment on every little detail of each other's beauty and take advantage of the general sour mood to go for walks round the neighbourhood.

'You're gorgeous. All the time, but especially when you're wearing black.'

'That's funny, I was just thinking that you're beautiful. But I wouldn't impose any sartorial conditions.'

'I'm always scared that you're coming back down to earth.'

'You're all I think about. I've been resisting the temptation to come up to your department and demand your full attention all day.'

And then, my father's birthday arrived. Joseph wanted to come to Rennes with me. We were going to spend our first night together. On the train, at his suggestion, I read *The Man Without Qualities* by Robert Musil, just like I'd once read *Life and Fate* by Vasily Grossman to please Igor. Every relationship comes with homework. During the party, he waited for me in a bar. I was afraid that he'd get bored, leave me and go back to Paris, so I wrote him texts under the table. And during dessert I received a *Let's get wasted tonight?* It's funny, because I remember this trivial message as the first instance of cognitive dissonance. I never get wasted. I don't have any particular family history with alcoholism, but I do have certain phobias. Among them, fear of flying, of ticks and of sleepwalking through a relationship. Being part of a couple whose value system no longer works, who encourage each other to make mistakes and then laugh as they both fall flat on their faces. I even replied: *Yeah sure!* But once I was at the bar, I couldn't do it. I'm hardwired to be in bed by nine-thirty with a Balzac novel. I spoke to him seriously and drank my pint with dainty little Marie Antoinette sips. The night of drunkenness didn't happen. The conversation wouldn't flow. After about twenty minutes, we went back to our medieval hotel with its romantic beams (or the other way around). I had the feeling that something had been played out that night. Joseph had seen me as too adult. As someone who would never let the roles be reversed. As an old lady who would end up scolding him and kicking him up the arse.

In Rennes, the next morning, before having the bright idea of drawing the curtains, Joseph and I fucked in the harsh light coming through the two huge windows to the left of the bed. Joseph, who is a regular consumer of porn, adapted to my less-than-inventive love-making method. This was how he discovered good sex with no frills. My speciality. A pelvic affair. Then, hotel rules being the same everywhere, we found ourselves in the street at eleven o'clock, heading towards the maritime museum. Unmotivated, weak-willed. So much so that on the way we stopped at a crêperie, Rennes's other speciality. We sat on the terrace at a wonky metal table. Next to us, a couple were eating with their heads down, while we made goo-goo eyes at each other. I said to Joseph that I wished I could reassure them: it was Adultery with a capital A having lunch next to them. Couples like us have an unbeatable topic of conversation at their disposal: the impossibility of their own situation.

What I didn't know yet, because I was an extramarital novice, is that this unbeatable conversation about the impossibility of being a couple can only be had a limited number of times. It's like a washing machine that you add a handful of screws to every time you use it. Eventually, the pieces of metal fly everywhere, destroy the motor and scratch up your face. This conversation, if it isn't resolved in the first three weeks, becomes a burden. If you start to exchange rebukes and criticisms before the decision of whether to be together has even been made, the possibility of an actual relationship is ruled out.

I learned later on, because they were on the same train back to Paris, that this couple having lunch next to us were also having an affair. Yann and Sophie had been working at the CAF, the benefits office, in Rennes for ten years. They had got to know each other physically while out on an assignment: they had to go together to give a slap on the wrist to a doctor in Finistère who'd been giving out too many sick notes compared to the national average, spreading empathy like the plague in Brittany. It was in a traffic jam on the way back, just on the way into Rennes, that things heated up. Yann reached over to get a bottle of water from the glove compartment, and his hand landed on Sophie's thigh. Two years had passed: their passion had lost its edge. On the train I also discovered that Yann was not at all the silent man we'd seen at the crêperie. On the contrary, he talked all the time. His words flowed continuously, undammed. We couldn't get one in edgeways. He plastered us, Joseph and me, with his conventional, unoriginal opinions. It was horrible. It ruined the journey back. (But if they're reading this, I'd nonetheless like to tell them that I was wrong to make fun of the pile of Chantilly on their crêpes. A lovesick anorexia is funny for two days, enough time to try it out and tell a couple of friends about it. But I lost ten kilos that year. I'm shocked by the family photos from the following summer: I'm surrounded by my children, and they're definitely mine, but I no longer have a mother's body. My arms look like two hosepipes.)

Before catching that train, Joseph had suggested we go find some other hotel rather than going to look at rope knots in a museum. I acquiesced. We wound up in a Kyriad by the station, which I now have to go past every time I'm going to visit my family in Brittany. We went into a bedroom with black and purple walls and *Star Wars*-inspired decor. In bed, Joseph asked me to tell him I loved him. Hard to refuse in that situation. I said, 'I love you,' even though I wasn't actually there yet. I think the fact he considers those words off-limits means he likes to hear them all the more. We left the hotel an hour later. I can still see him hurtling down the back stairs, his bag over his shoulder, exhilarated. He was just as happy to have a good story to tell as he was about the time we'd just spent together. In the foyer, he fabricated a family emergency as a pretext for giving back the keys. The death of a great-aunt. I was embarrassed and happy.

Newborns clench their fists around their heads. Nine-month-old babies blissfully reach towards the plug socket. We call this *behavioural development*, and it reminds us that we are a species. In the same way, when the 'lovers on a romantic getaway' stage is reached, humans always play with the idea that, if one of the two dies along the way, the affair will be discovered. Their life will be tarnished in the process, and the funeral very strange. Spare a thought here for poor Félix Faure, the president of France at the time of the Dreyfus affair. In the fourth paragraph of his Wikipedia page, we learn that he died while receiving fellatio from his mistress in the Salon Bleu of the Élysée Palace. On the way back to Paris, I was relieved not to have died in Rennes, and I had the smell of Joseph all over me, like a second skin.

*

But it was too late not to go mad. After we got back, I started to panic. I was no longer in control of anything. I felt like a swollen river bursting its narrow banks. I was crazed by the intensity of what I was feeling. Above all, I had a huge problem: whenever I looked at Joseph, I saw an incredibly serene man. He looked like he'd just come in from a stroll in the forest and was about to put the kettle on for a cup of tea. He was simply invigorated by what we were doing.

As for me: to understand what was happening inside my body, you'll have to imagine the cumulative trembling of the hands of all the pensioners in a nursing home. At the time, I couldn't explain this constant state of worry to myself. But it's likely that I was just starting to draw parallels between my incredibly strong emotions and Joseph's first declarations of his own cowardice. In addition, the guy was tying my head in knots by writing me rhythmic and subcontrary messages like *I'm afraid that you love me, that you don't love me, that you love me too much, that you don't love me enough*. What do you mean, you're afraid that I love you? Five minutes later, distracted by something else, I would put aside this actually very good question to let the sexual and emotional intensity grow even stronger. The important thing was to always be able to situate the other geographically:

Me: *Where are you?* Him: *In the office. Well nearly – I'm buying a sandwich.* Me: *Okay.* Him: *You?* Me: *Actually in the office.*

Me: *Are you in the office?* Him: *No.* Then: *I'll be there soon.* Me: *Okay.* Him: *Actually I'm there now.*

How long, still, until he'd be within reach?

Him: *I'll be there in twenty minutes according to the unions, forty according to the police.* Me: *I always believe the police.* Him: *That's journalists for you.*

One Tuesday, we spent the afternoon in a hotel near the office. It was my first time during work hours. I really liked the feeling of vulgarity that comes from walking into a hotel at noon. And from only using the bed as a surface, even though the hotel pompously offers a whole multitude of services. While we were having sex, Joseph told me that we weren't doing anything wrong. In the moment, I agreed. I nodded my head. It's true that we weren't committing anything too serious. Nothing calculated, anyway. Just a back-and-forth movement, universal and antediluvian. It wasn't harming or taking anything away from anyone. I didn't feel guilty. I hadn't yet realized that in time I'd pay for all of this. I remember the big white duvet, the walls in that taupe colour that interior designers all seem to eat for breakfast, and the insincere lovers' conversation: the sort where you dream up plans, where you gently tweak your political opinions, where you try to lend coherence to the incoherent path you're on. The sort where you transform the meagre four-page document languishing on your computer's desktop into the first draft of a book. Just to be able to say: my life is in motion.

Because at that time – maybe just to impress him, if I'm being honest – I was toying with the idea of writing a book about a racist Twitter troll. On the bed, we talked about it. Active in what we call the 'fasciosphere', Romain claimed to be a business-school graduate and passed for a champion of misinformation. But when I met him in a café in Saint-Germain-des-Prés, I found instead a young man with dishevelled hair. Romain trailed around Paris with his old student card, fake cashmere stoles and several plastic bags. He offered me gifts. He wrote poetry that wasn't too bad. Speaking to his family, I eventually learned that he'd been the victim of an assault, one night under the Eiffel Tower, which had damaged his brain, and that's when he'd become racist. It was an unfortunate consequence of his cognitive issues. Like in the film *Everyone Says I Love You*, where the son of Woody Allen's character, who has a blocked artery, starts voting Republican. What to do with Romain? Can you write about someone who's no longer really there? Smoking a cigarette out of the window, Joseph answered yes to this question. As far as he was concerned, journalists have to accept their own mediocrity. They feed off the vanity and ignorance of others, earning their trust and then betraying them. No way of getting a good article otherwise. It's always hard to say whether Joseph's advice – counter-empathetic, that of a big fish in a big pond – is good or very bad. But the book idea was abandoned three weeks later, when Romain was admitted to a psychiatric unit.

That evening, I left the hotel at six o'clock. I plastered a grin on my face as I came through the front door of my apartment and dived straight into the bathroom. I locked the door, took a shower, and then, wrapped in a towel, sitting on the floor, I read the message that I'd heard arrive from the bathtub.

I hope you have a nice evening being a respectable mother. They're lucky, these people who get to spend their evenings with you, with no effort, no scheming, as if it was normal. I want you to tuck me in at night, too, but no one gives a shit. I'm inconsolable when I'm not with you.

As I was falling asleep, I had the thought that, if we ended up together, I'd have to have a baby with him since he didn't have any. Mine were still young. Starting again would mean pushing back the dream of showering alone by however many years. I pictured it for a few minutes and that gave way to a nightmare: hundreds of tennis balls coming out of me. For how much longer would I have to brush the back teeth of little children?

*

According to my personal archives, it was during the final days of October that Joseph showed the first signs of withdrawing. All of a sudden, I don't know why, he was keen to make me understand that he wouldn't leave his partner. All the while continuing his *I love yous* and *I wanna fuck yous* on drip, he started to make horrible declarations under the horrible white lights of the places we'd have lunch. In a gourmet restaurant near work, in front of quirkily shaped plates and cutlery that we didn't know what to do with (since we hadn't actually felt hungry in several weeks), he started to shoot little jets of unpleasantness at me. With his index finger and thumb. Aiming at my forehead. Over the starters, he announced that he'd had a very nice message from his partner and that he was going to join her where she was currently on assignment. There was a public holiday coming up, so they were going to take the opportunity to spend the long weekend together. It was perfectly normal. So there you go, he was off to Metz for four days (the site of the *La traviata* incident).

Very nice message. Very nice message. Very nice message.

I was surprised that my plate, the microscopic portion of food on it, my designer chair and the floor underneath it weren't all immediately drenched in a pool of blood. I was wounded. Jealous. I was hurt that he didn't think our relationship – given its intensity – was the sort to call everything else into question. At the very least, the use of public holidays. On returning to the office, draped in my dignity, I sent him an email asking him never to speak to me again. *Give me some time. I'll come back to you. But I can't take it any more.* (No fear of sounding ridiculous.) It's one of the first of what I call my two-o'clock emails: those sent in the wake of a frustrating lunch. Joseph replied that he wanted to gouge his own eyes out for having hurt me. (An equal level of ridiculousness.) But he didn't recant. He stayed as resolute as a judge in Louisiana who, despite always being viewed as a humanist, has just handed down a death sentence.

So that's where we were. Now we see how men like Joseph take control of the situation. They lament the harm they do to the other person but claim that, while it's deeply regrettable, they can't do anything about it. It's the notorious responsibility without blame that we see in civil law. *Careful, don't take it the wrong way. If I've hurt you, it's not necessarily because I've behaved badly. It might even be the opposite.* Of course, this is false: what is true, and Joseph admitted to being one of them on that very first evening, is that there are men who live beyond their emotional means, who conduct love affairs without the necessary courage. To buy themselves some time, they declare the situation inalterable. An act of God. And instead of saying, *I don't want to*, they say, *It's impossible*. That day, Joseph responded to my sadness as if he had no way to act on it. As if he had no arms, no legs, nothing but a heart beating on a table. *Before this silence begins, I want you to know that I'm in love with you.*

Alas, this great silence, imposed by me and regretted a minute later, didn't last more than a day. And so, Joseph was very quickly able to have another go at this particular form of emotional cruelty. His little torture chamber was now a cut above in its methods of torment. Or, from another point of view, he was simply asserting his autonomy. This time, we were in a meeting room at the office when he told me he'd organized a romantic weekend away with his girl-friend. Two nights in a yurt in Normandy. It was necessary: maintaining his primary relationship would allow ours to go at its own pace.

'By the way, you look after Igor, too.'

In the moment, I kept quiet. I pretended to understand his story of precariously balancing the four of us. But I was spinning out all night, and, when I arrived at the office the next morning, I set about looking through the numerous websites offering such a stupid experience. I typed 'yurt' + 'Normandy countryside' + 'romantic' into Google. There were dozens of versions of the concept. For reasons that now escape me, I thought I'd found the right place, and, like a scorned woman dropping a mistress's red thong on the breakfast table, I sent him the link to the site in question, sneering at it. He was still asleep.

Thinking about it now, it was at this exact moment that I became an awful, bitter cry-baby. Abbreviation: ABC. Definition: victimized attitude that would make anyone go limp immediately, and which generally makes people fall out of love with you in a few weeks. That's what I'd become. I see myself in Berthe, Paul Signac's wife, whom he left for another woman. I read the book about her, smiling to myself, two years later. Charlotte Hellman, the great-granddaughter of the neo-impressionist painter, writes about her: 'The tender and sometimes tempestuous wife, even if she's fighting back as can be expected, becomes whiny and weepy; she does everything that should clearly be avoided, and falls into all the usual traps of the victimized woman: reprimands, tears, guilt trips.'

So that morning I was the 2016 version of Berthe Signac, since I'd written, at 9.03, a *Go to hell.* At 9.18: *I'm sorry, I'm not angry any more. Crying instead. Forget I said that.* The insult followed by flagellation. The erratic woman. Worst-case scenario. I was just missing the bucket on my head and manic cackle to pass for a total lunatic. For his part, Joseph now had confirmation that he could do anything he liked to me. Hundreds of billions of hours later, he replied that my messages that morning had made him furious. That they were impossibly malicious and, quite honestly, it seemed that I'd decided to wreck what we had.

Rereading his reply, years later, sends me back into an otherworldly rage. And if I was in such a rage at the time, it's because at that stage of our affair I could no longer sleep with Igor. I could barely bring myself to look him in the eye. I was angry because I was absolutely incapable of imagining a romantic spa-yurt-massage weekend, or any other similar nonsense, with my partner. Not because my relationship was in worse shape than his, as he seemed to think, but because I had, and still have, only one channel for my emotions, and he had overridden it in every possible way. I was angry because I could no longer see myself living without him, and I was now certain that he was destroying everything I had been building for the last seven years, all for nothing. Just to stash me away in the pantry, far away from the rest of the house. I wanted our relationship to speak or forever hold its peace. And then, I was infuriated because I was also starting to glimpse, stretching out before me, a long, non-negotiable recovery period. About the length of the affair times five. I was going to pay dearly for this.

When, one morning in November 2016, Donald Trump was elected president of the United States, Joseph was the first person I wanted to talk to. I'd rubbed shoulders with Trump's daughter Ivanka as a teenager, at an American tennis camp. One day I beat her at doubles: she's a very pretty girl, but she can't run. I mention this for the sake of History. The evening of the election, I got out the photos of her (badly shot, but in a swimming costume) that I'd been keeping for years in my pink Bugs Bunny kid's suitcase. I have lots of them because my mother would ask me to take some every summer. So, to please her, I developed certain strategies. I'd pretend to be taking a picture of the scenery and then put Ivanka in the viewfinder at the last moment. In one of these photos, she's looking at the camera: she seems to know what I'm up to.

Seeing her on every television in the world that morning gave me the impression of being absolutely minuscule. My epitaph: the girl who once briefly played tennis with Trump's daughter in 1995. Whereas, for two months, Joseph had put me at the centre of everything. The eye of God, or the camera of the great director of the universe, was always upon us and so close up that it had lost all perspective. After Trump's election, things were never simple again.

*

In mid-November 2016, Joseph and I both went to a party thrown by one of our colleagues, who's also my friend. It was a fancy-dress party. Jungle theme. It took place at her house in Asnières (on the same road where the Kouachi brothers, from the *Charlie Hebdo* attack, had lived). Inside, we found journalists, plastic tarpaulins on the floor, and old canapés. I was already very thin. All I was eating at that point was grated organic carrot and tins of albacore tuna. I was wearing leopard-print leggings. Joseph had thrown on a wooden necklace. That was his costume. He was happy to be there, especially when he discovered there was a guy there called Toussaint with pockets full of his favourite drugs. He followed him everywhere, gulping down shrooms.

At the end of the night, we sat down on the steps outside the house. Joseph pushed aside anyone within an arm's-length radius of us. He wanted us to be alone so we could talk the problem over again. With his partner, he had a home, commitment, loyalty, family, a team. With me... it didn't look so good. He was afraid of solitude: if we were together, I was going to be alone with my children some-times, wasn't I? What was he going to do, while I was doing that? He was also worried that my nature wasn't constant, and that I would treat him simply as a boyfriend, not a serious partner. This aside, he delighted in finding ways to say our names out loud together.

I have a memory of telling him that evening that his relationship with his partner reminded me of my uncle's inoperable brain tumour. I even specified 'vascular tumour' without really knowing what that was. It doesn't sound very nice, but I wasn't being mean: the first images that come to mind for me often have their own entries on Doctissimo. And anyway, I wasn't judging his relationship: we all have the right to confuse love with need. It's even charming, in old couples. Later on, after my uncle has died and we've said our goodbyes to him at Périgueux, I'll discover the word 'anaclitic' while reading a book on psychoanalysis, which corresponds well with the idea I have of the way Joseph weaves relationships with people: 'Anaclitic is a term used in psychoanalysis to describe the necessary dependence of a child on their mother. As the child needs their mother in order to develop, premature separation leads to a depressive syndrome called anaclitic depression. This term also describes a type of object relation in which the subject manifests a strong dependence on the other, an immense need for affection and an excessive need for understanding.'

Joseph feeds a single connection that is vital to him. Other attachments are left on the back burner: even if the relationship is important to him, he barely maintains it. I wasn't offering any of what was required to become his new strong, absolute connection, but the party in Asnières had made him want to conquer my personality. He'd been thinking a lot since, he told me, and he wanted us to go away together. A week later, I faked a reporting assignment and we spent four days in Maisons-Laffitte, in the Yvelines département just outside Paris. I chose it because my childhood best friend spent half the holidays there when we were little and it was the only place I was never invited. I had turned it into a paradise in my head. In reality, it's not a particularly interesting place. Just very clean and regular, with only two-storey buildings. Cold lighting in the Ibis hotel.

At the start of that first holiday together, the sudden closeness was a bit intimidating: you're brushing your teeth together and realize you don't actually know each other that well. But by the second day, we were getting into the rhythm of silence and conversation. We hired a Fiat and drove around the neighbourhood in it. We watched a programme about politics while drinking supposedly good craft beer. Played table football while downing madeleine-flavoured shots. Ate at the same pizzeria three times. Made love three times. We slept badly together the first night and not so badly the next. I rested my head on his torso when I woke up. By the third day, I missed him when I was away from him for eleven minutes in the bathroom. When I came back into the room there was a feeling of being reunited and an urgency to sleep together. I never got tired of his apprehensive way of seeing the world and all the intelligence that stemmed from it.

Walking through the gardens of the château designed by François Mansart, the highlight of the visit, Joseph told me that he wanted to be sure, before he committed to me, that I was a strong enough branch to hold him for the rest of his life; but he also told me – this was less positive – that he was already tired of thinking about everything he would have to do to make me happy. I, for my part, absolutely didn't hold back. I managed to unburden my conscience of the flaws I was discovering in him once we were back in our little grey car. Joseph had a rather high-brow way of speaking. He talked about art, science, politics. He was very meta. He could be unkind about other people (but his way of making fun of their pathos was irresistible: sometimes I'd still be laughing about a joke he'd made half an hour later). I had the impression that each time I'd tease him or poke fun at him, something lingered in the air afterwards. And then, he played at the hard-done-by white man so much that in the end he might as well be one. His true level of reaction (in the sense of being reactionary) was impossible to determine. As I wanted to take photos of this holiday, but I couldn't run the risk of having pictures of him on my phone, I took photos of silly things instead. A pebble he had touched. Or the côte de bœuf on his plate. The final night, as we were falling asleep, he said in a low voice: 'No point fighting it. You are in me now, I call you "my love", and it's tearing me apart.'

On the last day, while we were walking through the forest of Saint-Germain-en-Laye, Joseph made fun of me for using the present continuous to recount some uninteresting story. 'You should switch to the past tense. It'll be more straight-forward.' And then he stopped all of a sudden. He grabbed me by the waist and interlaced his fingers behind my back. A slightly rigid and unnatural position (bad choice from the director). Feet in the mud, he said: 'That's it. It's all over.' He was going to have to leave his partner because the idea of being without me gave him the sensation of having an empty cylinder where his guts should be. I could absolutely feel the void he was talking about. Situate it under the flesh. I had it, too, and I was pleased he was finally admitting to it.

But on the train, although he had said it was all over, it wasn't all over at all. Joseph's distant cousin, the one he was supposed to be on holiday with, called to tell him that his girlfriend was planning to come and meet him at Saint-Lazare station, and he needed to act quickly. I saw him panic. Hatch a plan. Call her and speak with a honeyed voice. Say, 'No need to come. See you soon, baby.' I couldn't believe it. My eyes darkened, but I didn't want to ruin everything. Everyone in the carriage was watching us: we were agitated, on the verge of tears. We seemed like lovers on the road to ruin. Joseph hung up. Without looking me in the eye, he said that the only thing he would regret was not having a baby with her. He added that, if he left her, she would disappear. Return to the Loire-Atlantique and never be seen again. He wouldn't survive it. Hope faded once more. We separated inside the train so we wouldn't arrive at the end of the platform together.

At the station entrance, the danger passed. I took his hand again and kneaded it. We went ten stops on the Métro together, pale-faced.

*

At the beginning of December 2016, Joseph spent ten days in Provence, at a mountain cabin with a swimming pool, with five friends from the same intellectual and bourgeois background as him. That did me in once and for all. At the start, he wrote to me a lot. Reassuring things. He wanted to walk side by side with me through the streets and to suddenly grab me by the waist. Feel my belly warm underneath his. Compress all of France, this great useless mass separating us. He told me how he pretended to be happy, lying on the lilo in the pool, but in reality he was only truly content when his friends agreed to talk about us. He needed to see me. Generally speaking, he was only happy when I was within, let's say, five feet of him. The rest of the time he was in a bad mood. He was reinvigorated when he knew he was going to see me. That need for proximity was the foundation of our relationship, he said, the way it functioned, fundamental to its development.

In the first days of his absence, I reconnected with my family. It was nice, even if I was trying to curb Igor's constant suggestions of going to the cinema, the only place in the world where he feels completely at ease and our only Saturday night activity, to the extent that I started to see cinemas as milestones along a mountain path where the summit is the end of our lives. I caught up on my understanding of my eighteen-month-old son's garbled words, and I listened to the older one, who would be four soon, divide the world into carnivores and herbivores. (What is this strange thing that's bigger than all of us? This vocabulary that springs out of nowhere. In *La Serpe*, the writer Philippe Jaenada is shocked that the insult '*bébé Cadum*', a scathing reference to the chubby, naked infants of the soap brand's long-discontinued twentieth-century adverts, is still used by children. It's an expression that, as an adult, you never hear anywhere any more. The most plausible, *dizzying* explanation, he writes, is that these words have stayed stuck in the playground. In that closed space, children have been passing them down for fifty years. We think they're insulting each other, but they're conserving a cultural heritage.)

I tried to not always have my phone in my hand. But I started to worry because bit by bit the rhythm of the messages slowed and their content dried up. Was I being too sensitive? I also found that, in the messages I was still getting, I was being increasingly associated with negative emotions. Joseph said that I wielded power over him. He was starting to realize it because Provence was outside my zone of influence. In Paris, what I was doing with him was tantamount to religious indoctrination. By the way, he'd watched an educational programme on France 3 about that: free will and alienation can coexist. I was like the Islamic State, and he was on the verge of being radicalized. The more time passed, the more he risked falling for my ideology. My presence would impose itself, invade him and destabilize him for eternity. Because I didn't realize it, but I was hurting him constantly. I said things that played on his mind for hours. I provoked jealousy and anxiety in him (emotions he'd banished from his current life). Essentially, my presence affected him, and not always in a good way. He wanted me to understand. *You can be in love with people who don't make you happy. You can love people who you can't see yourself spending your life with.* I triggered rumination and disquietude. *Don't destroy me pls.*

The word *destroy*, which I didn't understand at the time, takes me back to the writer Arthur Schnitzler, whom I discovered as a teenager through *Bertha Garlan*. The book tells the story of a woman destined to an equally depressing fate as that of Berthe Signac. The sort of woman who, after having had a rough day, realizes in the evening that it's been the same as any other. Her life consists of rolling around in the mud to reconquer an old flame from Vienna, a prodigious violinist, while her own status has passed from promising musician to a failed one. In the epigraph to *Dream Story*, a novella that he wrote much later, there's this aphorism which you can also find in discussions on the Aufeminin.com forum: 'If you think you're in danger of being destroyed by someone, before you assign them the full blame, ask yourself how long you were searching for a person like that.'

The last message I received, before the end of his holiday, was a *New York Times* article about Daesh. I was Daesh: he was sending me the latest news about myself. The message ended with a *take care* that would have been appropriate if ten years had gone by and we were meeting at Les Invalides for a coffee and reminiscing about the good old days. But here, it heralded the end. On his train home, he sent me a picture he'd just drawn from his phone. The profile of a sad man. All in yellow, or all in green, I don't remember. But all ill-looking. I received it during our work Christmas drinks. Just as I was dancing to Mariah Carey with three of my colleagues. I tried to carry on, to stay happy, to finish my beer, but it was impossible. I ended up on the sidelines of the party. I looked at the man's profile, his empty eye. I pushed down the rising terror.

We met up the next day, 12 December 2016, near the Assemblée nationale, where I was working for the day.

I hadn't managed to pay any attention to what the members of parliament were saying (even when everything's going well, it's not easy). At lunchtime, he arrived at the brasserie on the corner, La Dauphine, a good hour late and with his hair cut short. I have absolutely no memory of what he said to me. Afterwards, I crossed the Pont de la Concorde in a state of stupefaction. The Seine was smooth, people were strolling along leisurely, it seemed like nothing had happened. In front of the church on Place de la Madeleine, I called him: 'Start again from the beginning, please. I don't understand.' He said that he was suffering like crazy and he'd broken up with me. That's when the tears started to flow. He added that we could still kiss spontaneously, if the mood took us, but nothing more. Unplanned physical contact, yes – but no more talk of love. The idea of being a couple had to disappear. He was taking it off the table. His voice was steely, merciless. I hung up; no further sound would come from my throat. The closer I got to the office, the more my body deteriorated. The shadows under my eyes darkened, my hands were icy. In my head, Dany Brillant was singing a refrain that I wouldn't be able to shake for months: *Tu as brisé ma vie, tu as brisé mon cœur, tu as brisé mes joies. You've torn my life, my heart, my happiness apart.* I wanted to tell Igor everything, but I had to resist.

THE NEST

There are men whom you're destined to hurt whatever you say, leading you to freeze parts of yourself, and then there are men who are capable of hearing anything. Igor belongs to the second category. I did well to make him the father of my children – there aren't that many men in the second group, and I'm the sort of person who vocalizes everything. Who spills all her thoughts. 'Who has absolutely no filter,' says Igor's daughter. If only because my little truths can wash over him without causing catastrophe, I should really handcuff myself to Igor. Duct-tape both my hands to his belly. Or marry him.

Coming back from the Assemblée nationale, I wasn't going to last long without telling him about Joseph, especially as it was such a monumental event. I was going through my first real break-up, because it was the first time I'd been dumped while my brain was still in full-blown infatuation mode. It's different when you've moved past that into a more stable state. When you're capable of understanding and rationalizing what's being said to you. This, though – this was a trauma. I was the drugged-up dog abandoned by the side of the road. A buoy flung off a boat. A socket unplugged but still buzzing. A hamster who's been stuffed with sugar every day and then been told one day, quite bluntly, *no more sugar*. I was the last survivor of an extravagant balloon release: adrift in the sky, alone and with no future.

So the evening of the break-up, I went off to cry at *La traviata* in Metz (ultimately, I'd recommend it – to this day it remains the most intense musical experience of my life). The next day, arriving home in Paris, I yelled the words 'food poisoning' down the hallway in a very serious voice. I shut the bedroom door and flopped down on the bed. Pins and needles on my head. No juice left in my limbs. Struck dumb like a stretcher-bearer returned from the front.

It was a week later, just before the Christmas holidays, that I decided to talk to Igor. How to go about it? We'd just dropped our two children off at school and were sitting in the café across the street. I forced myself to turn pale. I stared off into the distance and pressed my lips together. It was the worried face I'd chosen to wear so that he'd ask me what was wrong. He asked. Now I had the impetus I needed. I said, 'I don't want to leave you. But I've spent the last three months madly in love with someone else.' Silence. I repeated myself. I stared at him. I back-pedalled, frightened by my own words. No braver than the next woman, I softened the truth with lies of different varieties. I pleaded his abandonment of the family home: that autumn, Igor had finished yet another book. He hadn't been there with us mentally. I reminded him of the four nights he'd spent in a Normandy hotel finishing it (I was clutching at straws here, I know). I assured him that I'd made my choice and that it was all behind me. I'd been caught up in it all for a long time, lost like a little pea in a big pot of sticky spaghetti.

The café window was all fogged up. The couple at the next table were watching us with curiosity. My throat was so tight with emotion that only the slightest trickle of air could get through. I feebly sipped at my coffee. If I had accepted the bit of croissant that Igor was offering me, I would have choked on it.

*

I confessed my affair, as I've just said, because I'm bad at keeping secrets. I don't know where normal people put them, but I have no corresponding interior space. Zero retention – the door is wide open. My older son says of his four-year-old brother, 'If you need someone to keep a secret for you, he's not your guy.' I'm the same. It was also because I felt that, at over fifty, Igor had lived long enough to know that, sometimes, people meet people – it happens. And finally, it was because I felt I was owed a debt equal in size to my confession: I thought Igor owed me because he had pulled me out of my normal life, the sort that our parents plan for us. At twenty-seven, I'd given up Jay-Z, his spiritual sons and the fantasy of growing impotent together with someone. In their place, I took the ageing hand of a grieving man. Crying in all the different places around Paris that reminded him of his wife. In front of the Odéon theatre. What's wrong? Oh, right.

Our relationship has lasted a decade now: when it started, Igor still had an AOL email address and it had only been a month since the death of his wife. He wasn't a happy widower, contrary to what a colleague, who we already knew was nasty before that, liked to say (another told me he was torn between contempt and disgust at the idea that we were already becoming a couple) – but it's true that we had got together during a hallowed time and that he never donned his mourning clothes. He wasn't the pale and lifeless widower that soothes everyone's conscience; the sort to grace the cover of *The Widower's Manual*, all drooping arms and hunched shoulders. Igor could have sold vitamins in the street. He was exuberant. Obsessive. Talkative. Caught by feelings of unreality. Getting hard to run away from death. Death catching up right as he's in the middle of it.

In those early days, I thought about fitting him with a set of toddler reins. He reminded me of a lawnmower gone haywire. He came and went from his apartment at all hours. Coddled his children, then suddenly left them alone. He wrote long, intimate emails to a Russian stranger. Drove a woman he barely knew to her doctor's appointment in the afternoon. He couldn't even explain it to himself; it was like all his ideas underwent a slight deformation before hatching. Some days I expected him to empty his bank account and disappear into the Rambouillet forest. Every twenty-fifth of the month, I would leave him and go to find some peace and quiet again. Eat prawns alone on my bed. But on the twenty-sixth, at eight-thirty in the morning, there he was before me again. Waiting at my bus stop. With his bike and his grey T-shirt, looking like a baby bird that's fallen out of the nest. So I stayed. I waited for him to calm down again. For him to set us up next to each other, his wife and me. I had to become his future without erasing his past, since Igor was caught between two adjacent worlds.

That whole time was troubling. In a dream dating from this early period, which I wrote down on my phone, Igor told me that he'd just been to see a journalist his own age, a revered war correspondent, to spend an hour in her arms and that, from now on, he'd be doing that every Monday evening. I imagined soft brown skin. A texture closer to his wife's, and surely better suited to consolation than mine. A few days before I fell pregnant, I woke from a nightmare which I added to the notes on my phone:

I tell Igor that we have to warn his wife that I live here because she could arrive any minute. He says no, her keys are from Zara, and, anyway, she'll let him know when she's on her way. I want to leave the house.

At dawn, when we were both awake and I repeated the dream out loud, Igor reproached me for giving voice to a fantasy that he wouldn't even allow himself. The next day, I took a note of this quote from an article in *La Croix*: 'If there is remarriage, for it to be a positive thing, it must come after the internal acceptance of the physical absence of the deceased.' That is not what we had done.

*

Of course, Igor didn't force me to do anything. I signed up for him, for all of it, and I would do the same again. Because our relationship replaced the other with no transition, like a sleight of hand, I now live with some anxiety. But if I'm being honest with myself, at the risk of coming across like

I was on the prowl for a widower, it's without a doubt *because* Igor was collapsing that I clung to him. It was his instability that intrigued me. His additional experience. And actually – it's easy enough to say it like this after the fact, but I think I needed to catch up on that surplus of life so I wouldn't remain a young girl forever, an *ad vitam* spectator of a man who had already lived his life.

So that's why I've never managed to feel guilty about my relationship with Joseph. For me, it's not about revenge, but balance. A logical twist to the story. That was the risk that he took. It was my turn. I fell in love with a man who allowed himself adventures, and, quite simply, I'd imitated him. I believe that before this, we weren't equal. And now we are, since these days both of us are likely to find our thoughts on someone else.

The day of my announcement in the café, we weren't there yet. I was still the thick-skinned young girl Igor had attached himself to one day because he needed to, and the father of my children was still sure of his domination. When I revealed my affair, he didn't lose composure in the slightest. He didn't let emotion get the better of him. He was just surprised that *that* was happening to him. He didn't think that *that* would ever happen to him. Now he was seeing himself anew, as a scorned man. A certified cuckold. 'Isn't that funny.' He ordered another coffee. He insisted on knowing his name. He insisted, but he was joking. He was joking, but he insisted. After all, he'd won, because I wanted to stay with him. Right? Right. He showed me videos on YouTube (the scene where the baker's wife comes home in Marcel

Pagnol's *La Femme du boulanger*) and cracked jokes: 'So from now on you're not to go to the toilet on your own any more, agreed?' Or: 'Even if it's over between you, do you think we could still ask him to look after the kids every other weekend?'

The same evening, he presented me with an iPhone. He dropped the box on the bed and said: 'Go on, take it, you good-time girl. You see, all you had to do to be showered with gifts was cheat on me.' He probably wanted to see the BlackBerry that had been an extension of my hand since the summer disappear. That was all. Case closed.

That was all, but everything had changed.

*

Before Joseph and the drinks on the third floor, for seven years, like in that Marilyn Monroe film, I'd been a big Igor enthusiast. It seems – I've forgotten, the way we forget the pain of childbirth – that he had me under his spell. That I let nearly everything slide. That everything about him entertained me. If Igor changed our one-year-old son's nappy in the middle of an awkward outdoor cocktail party, I thought him wild and liberated. I never found fault with anything he did. I was enthralled by his various incompetences. His flouting of social norms. His idiot-savant side. Enthralled by his conversation, full of backward somersaults, his quick comebacks, his imagination and his vulgarities. For example: at the time, Igor liked to tell me that if we broke up one day, all that would be left for me to do would be to put my Breton headdress on, head to Montparnasse station and go back where I came from like 'a slutty little teenage mum'. I don't know why such an outrageous joke made me laugh so much.

During this unconditional period, the proof of my compliance was that I cleared every overloaded plate he prepared for me: the amount of food I needed, times three. I gained eight kilos out of acquiescence. (If he could, Igor would spoon-feed us all: one day, he offered one of his son's friends a taste of a dish that was simmering on the stove, and before she could even say yes, he'd thrust the wooden spoon in past her tonsils.)

But since the affair, and since my children started to brush their teeth on their own – this series of emancipations – my outlook has evolved.

It hasn't been a catastrophe. This summer of 2019, ten years after we first met, three years after I met Joseph, is our best ever. The affair has become a simple fact of our history (a thought here for my friend who wouldn't stop saying, when I was at my lowest ebb, a phrase I found idiotic: 'time heals all wounds' – these days she alternates it with 'what goes around comes around'. I'll let you mull that one over). In the sun, his hair is white and his green eyes gleam almost yellow. In bed, his brown, granular shoulders remind me of the round rocks of Trégastel. His belly, which I've never found fault with, is still there. Well fed on tuna mousse and goat's cheese. I stroke it like an animal. We talk while his hands massage my buttocks. Igor is excellent at that: he traces pathways with his fingertips, rummages in the top of the intergluteal cleft as if it were a belly button, and never gets tired of it. We make love every other day and I'm surprised to find myself wanting him to stay inside me, an indubitable sign of the flame being reignited.

It's also this summer that the Anne Pingeot syndrome is confirmed. It's Igor who terms it that. In the first part of her collected correspondence with Mitterrand, the president's mistress seems submissive. A naive young girl, she's in awe of the great man. Classic romantic trope of the teacher and the student. Then comes the final section of the book. The moment where the power dynamic is subverted. Pingeot comes into her own, Mitterrand grows old. They reach a complicated age difference. Her forty years to his seventy. The president becomes imploring and nostalgic; she becomes powerful and ironic. That's what's happening to Igor and me.

So, this August, even though the other man is very distant by now, Igor is acting as if I'm always about to leave him. Possessive to the point of watching me do the washing-up.

'What are you thinking about?'

'About how washing-up liquid can be organic.'

'Really?'

'No.'

One evening, out on our bikes, he tells me that he doesn't know how he resists the urge to keep me tied up in a cellar somewhere. The next day, swimming in cold water, ankylotic and unhappy about it, he adds that it's going to take us a good fifteen years to get past this Mitterrandian imbalance. When I'm fifty and my body is taking its revenge for all the sport I don't do now, I'll be satisfied once again by the tanned seventy-year-old that he'll be (he refuses to understand the point of sun cream – the same way he refuses to understand that the more expensive an apartment listing is online, the nicer it generally is). The age difference between us will become unimportant once again. Maybe even invisible to others. Our curves of decrepitude, women's having a steeper gradient, will have crossed over. 'Oh, really, you think all that will still be true in fifteen years? You think that #MeToo is going to stop there, do you, Richard Gere?' I embrace him in the water. Always a bit surprised that he isn't more buoyant.

If Igor is worried these days, it's also because a friend's wedding proved to be an ordeal recently. Charlotte, my best friend from journalism school, got married to a corporate lawyer who looks like a twenty-year-old Bob Dylan. A young man who stays fresh, despite his escapades in Berlin, and who wants his wife to look after herself as well (what kind of *pressure*, honestly – having to maintain your freshness under the watchful eye of someone effortlessly fresh). They got married at his family home, a Provençal farmhouse with a dark-blue swimming pool. The kind of house where you eat artisan mozzarella for breakfast and leave your empty coffee cup behind on the table because there's a lady who'll come and clear it up after you.

At this three-day wedding, there were ping-pong tables, euphoric cicadas, and a good dozen thirty-something guys born to wear Ray-Bans. Tall. Clever. Well dressed. Good dancers. Igor, who knew some of their parents, couldn't stand their music, which he didn't even know the name of. He said techno instead of electro. The waistband of his red swimming trunks was too loose. He took me by the waist and called me 'Maman' as a joke. The young men, who'd all taken amphetamines, were throwing carnivorous looks at everyone and sometimes at me. The whole weekend, Igor seemed to me like he could have been Charlotte's uncle, and he noticed.

'So, you're sure you wouldn't rather be with some top-less guy who drinks spritzes by the pool and has his own podcast?'

'No. Well, I don't know.'

The feeling isn't new. Charlotte has always treated Igor like he's her favourite uncle. The difference is that, at the start, this aroused my suspicion. Generally speaking, I found that she gave herself the right to touch him more than if he had been our age. While, of course, every part of his doughy body emitted violent erotic charges. One evening, in her student apartment, I had to remove her hand, which had been resting for too long on his arm. I couldn't bear it. When I did that, they both looked at me, as shocked as if I'd let out a blood-curdling scream. I thought that after that unhinged gesture, I had the choice between an embarrassed smile and totally losing it. Getting up and pouring a bottle of wine over her head. Being shunned from society and becoming a recluse. (I'm aware that there's something pretentious about dropping Kafka into my story. But I often think, in moments of potentially losing it, of this extract from his diary: 'Were we crazy? We ran through the park at night, swinging branches.')

Ten years later, it's perhaps temporary, but the irrational anxiety has switched sides. I no longer monitor Igor's arms, while I see him watching closely if I engage in the slightest conversation with a young dad on the beach.

*

At the start of our relationship, I was jealous in the extreme. Igor was forty-seven and presented a magnificent spectrum of grey, with his hair one shade and his usual clothes another. His physical strength hadn't yet begun to diminish. He would carry me on his shoulders up to the sixth floor of my building. Every day, he received Facebook messages from girls trying their luck with the B-list celebrities he appears with on TV – there are a lot of them. He was pursued by a nymphomaniac with the surname of a German astrophysicist. He was outrageously familiar with everyone, which made me possessive. But above all, I was jealous of his wife, whom Igor never criticized. In the thread of his years with her, there were only bright colours. Red, green, blue. Stop. I arrived after this beautiful rainbow and had trouble finding my place. The Joseph affair has somewhat eclipsed those heavy years, to the point where it's increasingly difficult to remember them. But I remember nonetheless.

February 2012, in Israel, an argument. We were coming back from the Dead Sea (Igor, suddenly understanding Lacan, thinks that it's the name of the sea that sparked the argument). The whole day had been murky. It's a huge puddle, the Dead Sea. And the hotels are full of salty-skinned old people moving very slowly. I was pregnant with our first child. In our air-conditioned hire car, on the road back towards Tel Aviv, I explained to him that just because his wife was dead, it didn't mean that I didn't have the right to some superlatives as well. He couldn't refuse me them all with the excuse that it wasn't kind to her. He could choose some for me too. Even bizarre or false ones. 'I've never met a thirty-year-old girl with such an extensive vocabulary as yours,' or 'I've never touched an arse that's so firm and so soft at the same time.' I told him to sort himself out.

In those first years, all I heard, from what he told me about his wife, was what differentiated her from me. And each characteristic crushed me. Sportier. Thinner. More passionate about politics. More socially aware. More energetic. And me? I was more what, then? One moment I'm particularly ashamed of: in our new apartment, unpacking boxes of books with Igor. I ask, 'All these books are yours. Where are hers?' I want to hear him say that this shared interest is something that belongs to us, something specific to our relationship. 'Oh, would you stop already? Hers are in that box over there… I shouldn't even respond. What are you implying? What is this – what do you even know about her?!' Answer: nothing. The refraction of your refraction. I know ten anecdotes, and not even the sound of her voice.

When our first son was born, I was the average age for French women to have a baby, but in every other sense it was too early. It was three years after her death, and it uncovered a gaping wound. None of us really knew what we were doing. And becoming a mother immediately exacerbated my rivalry with Igor's dead wife. At the time, when he hadn't yet locked all his devices, while his back was turned, I'd type her name into the search bar of his emails. I'd read everything he had to say about her to other people. The next day, I'd make my apologies. He'd tell me off: 'That's such a violation, you know.' When he'd calmed down again, I'd ask him to tell me more about her. To unbury his grief a little. But he never would, and I think I admire him for that – making his sadness a topic of conversation with me would have ruined it.

The year 2012 was also when Igor's eldest, his daughter, moved out. Her brother stayed. In the damp duplex that we didn't much like, there were now four of us. Of which three were unhinged: a baby, a teenager and a first-time mother. Up until then, at the first sign of familial tension, I'd been able to escape to the cinema. Or go and drink three glasses of wine. What I hadn't anticipated was how the arrival of a baby was going to chain me to the apartment and its immediate surroundings. Never again would I be able to go out without giving it some thought first. It was a sudden drop in freedom (like a sudden drop in temperature). And because of the close quarters, like in a reality TV show, the teenager and I took on fixed roles. Him, the careless slob turning the TV up too loud and trailing Babybel wrappers; me, the nagging shrew inspecting the fridge: 'You haven't eaten my prawns again, have you?' A bitter, tired character who would never get, from Igor, an 'I know it's not easy for you to find your place' or a 'What can we do to make you feel better?' (the foundation of non-violent communication). Instead, when I complained, he would just shout 'Fuck!' down the phone at me.

It was the millionth dramatic and desperate fight about his son that sent me to therapy for the first time. On the second floor of an old Parisian building, going into Madame A.'s office, the first things I noticed were an artistic taste and hair colour both absolutely identical to my mother's. The cushions illustrated by an Argentine painter we both adore, the dark colour of the parquet, the old accordion on top of the piano. My aesthetic attachment was very strong, and I didn't know if this would be a good thing for transference or not. Years later, I'd have the chance to contemplate all that twice a week, because she would become my psychoanalyst. The one who'd listen to me purge Joseph from me, bit by bit. But we're not there yet. That's a problem for another decade. At the start of the 2010s, she had a different mission. It was in her consulting room that I understood that, if Igor's wife was a concept to me, to her family she was an absent body.

REPORT FROM THE FIRST SESSION

Igor's son needs a psychological adoption. You have to say yes to him before you say no. You behave like an annoyed big sister or a nag, although a mother can nag as well, but it puts you in an absurd position. He is in limbo, you mustn't expect anything from him, and it's all probably temporary. You certainly mustn't call Igor as your witness on this. He has a lot of responsibility towards his son, notably to protect and further him. The more his son crumbles, the more he'll lay it on thick to save him. It's here in this room that you can speak your problems aloud.

So that's what I did. The situation improved. But the truth is, the boy and I began to love each other indisputably when he got his own apartment. Between us, these days, there's no grand declaration of love. Just his arm around my neck and a kiss on my cheek when he says goodbye. His feet plonked on my knees while he watches TV. His way of coming and lying on our bed for a chat while Igor and I are in it. Of our whole family, there are certain questions that he'll only come to me with.

As for his older sister, the first time I met her was strained. A year hadn't yet passed since the death of her mother. We were in the garden of the house in Beauce. The whole day, she kept a right angle between her gaze and mine. It was masterful. The third time we saw each other, she was different. She'd laid the table for dinner because I was coming over. Two memories of our life together. I remember one morning at breakfast, when she was wearing a very short nightie. She sat herself on her papa's lap. She was physically stunning. Boobs and hips for days. Buttering my Krisprolls, with my broken elbow, I thought: *Okay, so I live with Brigitte Bardot now*, and also: *What the fuck am I doing here?* I also have in mind the evening when I told her I was pregnant with my first son. She was sitting on her bed in the darkness. She said, 'I wasn't sure if I would be pleased. But actually, it's clear to me that I love him already.' She got up to hug me.

It's frustrating, I can't even describe how much I love that girl. How about this: she's the one I want to walk over the plastic floors of my life. When I'm covered in tubes and hooked up to machines in a hospital room, it's her footsteps I'll want to hear approaching. She'll bring me a kiwi smoothie and celeb magazines. Our chit-chat will make me forget the noise of the thousands of TVs that, now they're all digital and mounted on arms, practically touch the patients' faces. She is eight years younger than me, and I'll also be impatiently waiting for her to visit my retirement home in the countryside outside Paris (if, in fifty years' time, they *still* haven't built the nice family-sized retirement cottages on the Atlantic coast I dream of). Just recently, Igor's daughter went to view an apartment whose balcony looks out on our own. The boys suggested we could join them together with concrete. That suggestion proved decisive. She took the apartment. Some of my friends find this strange, but I can't wait for there to be a child in there for me to look after. What else could I do with my existence, other than to continue to build, like her, a family of us all? When I thought about leaving Igor for Joseph, for those few weeks of my life, it was the idea of leaving these grown-up children behind that terrified me most of all.

*

The whole thing brought me closer to them. Because, after loving me, Joseph left me. And, by leaving me, he drove me insane. Which sent me to the psychoanalyst. After a certain amount of time, without knowing if it was down to the treatment or to time (that's the charm of psychoanalysis), I moved on from him. And, at the same time, my relationship with Igor changed. Ever since I worked out how it's formed, his personality jostles me less, and I have realized that I appreciate its constancy.

There you go. Now I know that I live with a neurotic cockerel, hen-pecking us all, and I make do. Where his loved ones are concerned, his fears are as follows: that we might ever be deprived of any food; that we might get too hot and, consequently, get sweaty and dirty; that we might be poisoned due to the fridge's cold chain breaking; that our phones might run out of battery. This spurs him to prepare a hundred dishes every evening, to count how many layers we're wearing ('Take off your sweater, the sun's come out again') and to constantly remind us to shower. When he wants to put a wash on, he'll pull your socks right off your feet while you're reading peacefully on the sofa.

My older son and me, one morning, in his bedroom:

'I wish I could wear my football shirt.'

'You can wear it on Wednesday, when you've got football.'

'No, Papa's coming to pick me up.'

Knowing looks; the conversation ends there. We both know you can't wear polyester satin around Igor. It's too warm.

Additionally – and all this is connected – Igor is a man plagued by catastrophic scenarios. At the moment, every other morning I get a jet of icy water to the face when I turn the shower on. *For fuck's sake, he's turned the boiler off overnight again.* I try to work out where my children are to see if I can cross the hallway in the nude. I drip on the parquet, which turns dark from the water. I dash into the kitchen. Turn the boiler back on, end up feeling afraid of it myself. I run back the other way. 'It'll be winter soon. We're going to have to think about being brave again, Igor. We can buy a second carbon monoxide alarm, if that makes you feel better?'

Finally, apart from the cinema, Igor's favourite activity is reserving train tickets. Lying on our bed or on the sofa, he compares prices and journey times on the SNCF website without anyone having asked him to. Like he's a travel agent undergoing training for a new reservation system. He puts in different options, re-examines them, and expects to be applauded for it every time.

'If I get you this ticket, that means you can leave Paris at noon.'

'Yes, honey, but that's too early. I've got a phone meeting at eleven.'

'Are you sure? At eleven? Well, why don't you go straight to Montparnasse and do your phone meeting from there?'

'I don't feel like it. I'd rather leave in the afternoon.'

'That's silly, isn't it? It's more expensive. I only buy off-peak tickets these days.'

'Can you let it go, please? I'll sort it out myself.'

'Okay, come on, I'm not telling you what to do. I'm just asking you to consider doing your phone call from the station. That way you can leave Paris two hours earlier. You'll have time to spare, no stress.'

'No.'

'What about the one o'clock train, then?'

His pleasure lies in selecting the right choice from a multitude of equally good alternatives. By the way, I get it now: Igor struggles with conversations that don't put his algorithmic capacities, his iterative mind, into action. That's just the way he is. His nightmare: having a dull day at work recounted to him. His eyes grow wide and glaze over.

*

Our best summer is behind us. In this autumn of 2019, the last dinner of Rosh Hashanah unfolds almost like the others. After the prayer, Igor devours two poppy-seed bagels, relishing them a little more than usual: he has to lower his cholesterol, these are the last indulgences before his diet begins. Then he begins his toing and froing from the kitchen, so he doesn't have to sit down and listen to us. When the main course is over, his favourite part of the meal, he takes himself off to play chess on his phone. We see his shoes sticking out from the sofa.

That evening, we argue like in the good old days. I tell him off for his lack of interest in us all. He tells me off for not giving a shit about helping to prepare the meal. Which is true. He's the one who bought the mortadella, cooked the beef with carrots, and the lemon chicken, *and* who laid the table with his wedding crockery. The set that lives in the cabinet – her cabinet. As usual, I'd behaved as if I were a guest. A tad dishonestly, I try to explain to him how all the fuss of the high holy days always makes me feel like a usurper and that's why I do as little as possible and don't even sit next to him at the table. I put myself with the children. I don't want to take his wife's place – physical, symbolic or administrative. I say all the time that that's what stops me from envisaging us getting married, though actually I've never had any interest in getting married. But perhaps Igor is starting to get tired of hearing it.

Since my affair with Joseph, I thought I'd been definitively cured of my jealousy concerning Igor. Until this Sunday, when we went to pick up our youngest son from a birthday party in Aubervilliers. A woman arrives, about forty-five, with very short hair. She's wearing a beige raincoat and high heels. She slinks into the lounge like the bombshell from *Roger Rabbit*. Then she slips her coat off over her arms. She's wearing a green sequined dress. Sitting down, her legs crossed, you can see her skin up to her mid-thigh. She has freckles on her knees. Weird. When she starts to speak, I think that she's the precise level of stupid that gets some men going. By which I mean, the way she talks gets on your nerves without being entirely unbearable.

I see Igor fidgeting. To put up a front, he catches the four-year-old birthday boy by the arm (practically knocking him off his feet) and pops him down in front of him. It works – she's watching them. He starts ruffling the boy's hair and very loudly telling him a story he's making up on the spot. He plucks the boy's little pink box of bubble-gum from his hands and juggles with it. It's too much excitement at once, the box falls to the floor. He picks it up again, all the while continuing to yell his story. Later on, in the garden, he peppers an anecdote that I know well with ludicrous embellishments. Then he gets passionately involved in a conversation about Line 14 on the Métro (which Green Dress takes every morning). I'm in a bad mood. I don't even want to try to remind him of my exist-ence by intervening in the discussion. I just murmur, 'Stop peacocking, please. You're out of control,' and I speed up our departure.

I sometimes wonder if Igor has cheated on me, too. Every time he replies, 'And when would I do that, exactly?' His ideology is that you shouldn't say anything, as long as you haven't decided to leave yet. But that evening, while we're eating spicy prawn spring rolls, he admits, 'Earlier, it's true, I got worked up like I hardly ever do.' I ask him if that happens to him often. He tells me that the last time was with a woman working at the cinema. Igor had warned me that grief had taken something away from him which would come back with the fear of growing old: 'Watch out, I'll cheat on you the day I become a grandfather.'

I'm still waiting for that day, and as for me, for the moment I've given up affairs. They eat up your headspace. There's nothing left for your professional *drive*, as we say in psycho-analysis. It involves too much screen time. It makes you less present with your children. It makes you fall out with your friends, who are afraid for you, or jealous (it's not entirely clear). It distracts from the climate crisis.

So I imitate my friend Vincent and I try to indulge my narcissism without going too far. Low-key seduction during weekday lunch hours, which you'd think had been invented for the purpose. I could be content with that if I didn't keep landing such idiots. Antoine, the police superintendent who decided to hit on me by negging me incessantly – he tells me that I don't deserve the information he gives me because I don't work fast enough. Jérôme, the most recent to date, a television journalist. For an hour and a half, this guy talks at me with his mouth full about the urgent need to sell his family château in the Gers because the heatwaves coming in the next decade threaten to lower its value. Collapsologist property speculation. *Things are pretty tough for you, eh?*

So, for now, it's Igor for life.

2029. Our children are seventeen and fourteen. Igor, sixty-six, is retired. He's writing a book about the streets of Paris with Loràht Deutsch, whose coronary artery has finally been unblocked. I'm forty-six. Newspapers are now extinct. I'm writing a novel that switches between Igor's grandmother, deported to Bergen-Belsen, and my grand-father, who had been in Marshal Pétain's security detail (before rejoining the underground). We live, like everyone of our social class, in a house in the inner suburbs of Paris. My youngest son and I have finally got the dog we've been asking for for ten years. We warm our feet underneath him. Igor complains that he's the one who walks and feeds him. We pretend to sympathize. We don't fly more than once a year. It's been restricted by law. We know now that one puff of a vape is more harmful than ten years' exposure to asbestos. Several friends have died from it.

2039. Igor is seventy-six and I'm fifty-six. If all has gone according to Igor's plan, I no longer look at other men. I'm content to admire his sparkling colours. If all has gone according to the children's plan, the elder has become a pro-fessional footballer and the younger, a painter who unleashes his *destructive anger* on the canvas and lives in a house with several dogs (like Maria Callas in her final years). Thanks to their success, Igor and I have re-entered the city walls. We've moved into a house in Montmartre. Every morning, while he's walking the dog, Igor touches the breasts of the Dalida statue while murmuring 'boobs' three times.

2049. Igor (eighty-six) and I (sixty-six) both have serious neck problems. It was predictable. Igor has always put on weight around there. And I have an anatomical defect in that area. Like all my Breton ancestors, I have a line that rises too sharply from the top of my neck to my chin. It's like a taut washing line. Thirty-seven years after her death, I'm thinking of Nora Ephron and her book *I Feel Bad About My Neck*, in which she talks about the cost of keeping up appearances as we grow old. 'Our faces are lies and our necks are the truth. You have to cut open a redwood tree to see how old it is, but you wouldn't have to if it had a neck.'

2059. I'm seventy-six. In my bed, I hum 'La Strasbourgeoise'. A military song we've all sung together a thousand times in the car and whose penultimate verse still gives me shivers:

> *Gardez votre or, je garde ma puissance,*
> *Soldat prussien passez votre chemin.*
> *Moi je ne suis qu'une enfant de la France,*
> *À l'ennemi je ne tends pas la main.*

> Keep your gold, I'll keep my pride,
> Prussian soldier, don't break your stride.
> I'm a child of France and France only,
> I won't shake hands with the enemy.

*

Do you think the places where our lives' key moments happen recognize us? One beach knows mine and Igor's story well: the Plage des Vieilles, on the Île d'Yeu. It was on those sands that I learned he'd been widowed. I see us there again, my friend Charlotte and me, in July 2009. She was reading the paper. In her right hand, in extreme close-up in my memory, she was holding both a cigarette and the obituaries page. I thought it was too hot to be smoking. I was lying face-down on my towel. She let out a strange noise. I lifted my head up to look at her. She read me the death notice.

We had spoken about Mozart and Salieri in his office a week earlier, but I didn't know that Igor was married. When I got back to Paris, I sent him a message of condolence on Twitter. A short sentence that took me an hour to come up with and that I find affected now. *All my thoughts in such a difficult time*. He came back to my office three weeks later. I was wearing a thin green woollen dress (see, we can all wear green dresses) and a straw hat. I was surprised to see him again. When I caught his eye in the corridor, he was talking to the managing editor. He gave me a sign: his finger tracing circles to say, *I'll come to see you afterwards*. Ten years after that spiral in the air, one weekend in September, Igor and I arrive at that same beach. He tells me there's no point telling him again about that day with Charlotte and the newspaper: he knows, both of us think about it every time we approach the sand. Before he takes the kids out kayaking, we talk about our beginnings again. I'm surprised to find myself crying. I still have so much anger towards him for pulling me into his life so early and forcing me to commit, despite myself, such huge violence against his children, who saw me in the marital bed when they walked past the bedroom. And I'm angry with him for then acting like he needed to protect his son from me, while I was so unwell myself.

'The Plage des Vieilles knows all our drama,' as Igor would put it.

Other than our office building, it's the Rue de l'École-de-Médecine that knows the most about me and Joseph. The first time we had lunch in the only café on that street, we started to fall in love. We'd stopped there after the morning we spent in the Jardin du Luxembourg. As I walked away afterwards, I said to myself: *If he's fallen for me, I'll get an email in the next hour*, and I did. *I miss you already. No one talks the way you do.* The second time we had lunch on that street, it was just after his exhibition in Hungary. He was passing through Paris. We met there because it was where our respective Métro lines crossed. By then, all that was left of our relationship was a shared secret vocabulary and an excessive consumption of tobacco.

And then there's the Rue Charles-François Dupuis, right by République Métro station, which knew me at sixteen, when I hung around there with my friend from Neuilly-sur-Seine. Her boyfriend, a little older than us, lived there. He worked in a record shop. When we went to see him, we felt worlds away from the ridiculous families and the thousands of trees (one tree per 4.5 residents) in our bourgeois suburb. It's in the café on the corner of this street that two decisive encounters will take place for me. At the end of 2019, I'll make the acquaintance, within a week, of a once-famous actress and a feminist comedian who, between them, will give me an idea. And it's thanks to this idea that, after a painful prolongation full of further ignitions and disappointments, the Joseph era will come to an end.

THE CAGE

Despite working in molecular science, my aunt has always had the psyche of a film star. When she was little, she couldn't understand why the Virgin Mary had been chosen to be the mother of God, rather than her. She was scared of becoming too beautiful and people only loving her for her looks. At forty, she was an atomic bomb. At sixty, she hasn't changed. She has always careened without warning between extreme rationality and eccentricity. On Christmas evenings, she talks about 'radiation chemistry' and then undulates her body in the centre of the living room as if no one were watching. My favourite memory of her is at a family reunion in the Cantal; I was twelve years old. Out on the porch, she told me about the passionate affair she'd had when her son was a year old. She'd left her perfect husband, who'd made her happy for years, for a guy who'd made her roar with laughter during a seminar on hard sciences: 'I went from a plump little housewife whose world revolved around her baby boy to a skinny woman in love.'

It was seeing, a few days later, the father of her child from below (he was up on a stepladder changing a lightbulb) that made her realize she had to pack her bags: 'I was completely swept up in it. All of a sudden, I was ready for whatever would happen, and I told myself my son would adapt.' She took a little apartment and made multiple back-and-forth car journeys to Germany to see her new lover. One time, she arrived unannounced, wanting to surprise him, which she did – in bed with another woman. She cried the whole way back: Potsdam, Brunswick, Dortmund, Charleroi, Compiègne, Paris. It took her seven years to get over it, and she never loved so violently again.

After the break-up at the Assemblée nationale and my confession to Igor, she was naturally the first person I thought of. I expected her to tell me that my separation from Joseph was a blessing. I texted her, saying I needed to see her urgently. Imagining the worst, my aunt had me come to the National Centre for Scientific Research to see her the very same day. The only colour for a mile around: the geraniums of her office. She was sitting in her leather armchair. Well? I told her the whole story, in order. I was boring even myself, but she didn't interrupt me. To end, I told her I'd been getting ready to leave everything behind, like she'd done, but Joseph had thwarted my plans.

'We're in love, but he's pushing me away because he doesn't want what he feels for me to take root and seize control. He can't imagine us living together. Mostly because he envisages me throwing dishes at his face. When all I really do in the evenings is take baths.'

She burst out laughing.

'Oh, but that's nothing. Just the melodramatic way people in love have of thinking…'

I was gobsmacked – she seemed not to remember the moral of her own story. She didn't tell me to go home and try to forget about it, but, on the contrary, to salvage the situation.

'You just need to calm him down! If you're in love with him, you're not obliged to buy his story of mutual destruction. You can still keep each other a while longer. This happens to everyone. C'est la vie, darling.'

'Really?'

'Yes, really! You know, we're all subject to the forces of attraction. We're no different than atoms. Simply put, you need to take some time to think about it. You didn't come here for a lecture on morality, did you?'

(Yes.)

'No! But I didn't think you'd tell me to reject the break-up.'

Pleased to see me and to hear that my news was apparently nothing serious, and lacking knowledge on the subject of Joseph, my aunt made the same interpretative error that day as I had early on in our relationship. The following winter, she would finally understand my lover's personality – and she would tell me to run a mile. But at that point, she couldn't imagine that he really believed we were heading towards the destruction of our respective relationships and then ourselves, in that order. *Hahaha – but no, really.* And that's how, once again, Joseph's immense capacity for self-preservation was overlooked. Who will listen to this man, who will understand what he wants?

Not me: it's still too early and I've got my own problems. I'm his opposite – pure passion, ready to be shaped and fired at a thousand degrees. And when that happens, which isn't very often, I'm one of those people who don't let anything hold them back. I don't negotiate with moral values. I don't have any, anyway. It's like I've been raised in the jungle. I'm okay with the strange and the ill-advised. With pressing the button that reshuffles all the cards. Or the one for big explosions. I'm up for the widower, the orphan, the megalomaniac and the depressive, as long as he's interesting. The adolescent crisis, which I never had, is brewing. My lack of restraint feels simultaneously heroic and overwhelming to me. I said goodbye to my aunt at six o'clock, and we hugged each other tight. I went down the stairs as fast as I could, enjoying the spectacular return of my motor function. I was back on my feet again. I wouldn't give up. I wouldn't admit that, in life, it's entirely possible to pull the plug on passion, even when it's at its very height.

I was thirty metres away from my building when I realized that it was impossible to go home right away and put on a normal face. I paused in the café where they play the news channel on a big screen, which always strikes Igor and me as a disproportionate honour. But at least you can see properly. Cristiano Ronaldo was receiving the Ballon d'Or. It was sitting there, two weeks after our break-up, turning the plastic stirrer round and round in my *menthe à l'eau*, that I cooked up my desperate riposte. Quite quickly, a word came to me, humbly inspired by the thawing of the Cold War: detente. I summoned Joseph by email: *Let's meet in an alley near the office. I have something to say to you.* The next day, after work, we were face to face. He was wearing a new navy-blue peacoat that I could tell he was proud of.

What will she think of my new navy-blue peacoat? My hands were all over the place as I explained why we had to go back on this brutal separation. Keep seeing each other. Just calm down, and stop asking the big questions of life together. Look, it wasn't even that complicated:

'We take it slow, we see what happens, we call it a detente.'

I didn't raise my eyes to look at him until this last word. His smile reached his earlobes.

'If someone had told me that I was going to get you back today…'

On our way back to the office, we walked a metre apart. Together we took up the whole width of the pavement. The air between us was alive. Fizzing and warm. As we passed the entrance, we were in slow motion; it was like a triumphant comeback. I clenched my fists with joy, but I didn't realize the extent of our misunderstanding. For me, the detente was our relationship continuing, just taken down a notch. Joseph, who has never known moderation, thought that he now had the green light to pick it up, and drop it, whenever he wanted to. Alternating sex and silence to stop any romantic escalation. A good technique. But how long before we'd self-destruct?

Less than a month. Our relationship was back on its feet, but it had thrown its back out. All we talked about any more were painkilling treatments. It was tedious for everyone. And, in particular, Joseph was now behaving like a geisha. In this second phase, he gave in to some of my demands, poked his head into my office if they didn't arrive when expected, but held back from making any propositions himself. He never sent spontaneous messages any more. The words that I inspired in him, which just two weeks earlier had reached me as regularly as your head breaks the water when swimming breaststroke poorly, were put away.

Now Joseph let several days pass before replying to my emails. Or even (come on) he didn't reply at all. Because I was in love – and even with that aside, because I pay such close attention to the psychological state of those around me (it's my strength and my weakness) – my overactive emotional detector was picking up the contradictory vibes he was giving off at 1,000 per cent, and I was permanently anxious as a result. It was hellish. I felt like I could set him alight just by brushing against his knee, but also that the force of him pulling back would be irreducible. He pushed me away even though he wanted me. Gave me a non-verbal yes and a verbal no. Depending on the day, came by or didn't come by my office. If he was emotional, he wanted to throw those feelings away. Thought of me a hundred times without telling me. Hadn't replied to my last text, but said: 'We should have sex.' Then disappeared.

For André Green – psychiatrist, psychoanalyst and philosopher of the negative, a title I envy – there exists a normal negativity of the psyche when its demands aren't immediately satisfied, and another, more radical negativity: when the drive emanating from the subject – Joseph – is strong and its object – me – proves too unpredictable, a disengagement takes place. The subject–object connection isn't broken: it's the engagement with the drive itself that is undone. That's exactly what was happening – the drive was gone! In Green's book *The Work of the Negative*, there's an entire chapter on this disconnection of the subject. Fascinating pages, once you've experienced it, which explain how the subject cuts off his drives to defend himself from what the object could want to make him undergo. Enslavement. Possession. He confuses what he wants to do to me with what he risks happening to him. He opposes it with an imperative and irrevocable no: 'In general, the anxiety aroused by the drives, the fear of rejection and the loss involving interminable pains of mourning, rage, devaluation, apprehension of intolerance to frustration, drive the subject to refrain from responding to the object's advances, or even to frankly discourage them or to flee from all situations of closeness.'

In a few weeks, Joseph had reduced my existence to only the moments when I was physically there in front of him. I asked him why he didn't message me any more. *I thought I needed to keep you at a distance, but actually the distance is already there. We need to be happy without each other as well, since we've decided not to be together.*

*

I wasn't lying that evening when we first met: I really like Boulogne-sur-Mer. And for the Christmas holidays of 2016, which would punctuate the detente, I had insisted on renting a house in Wimereux, the seaside resort one town along. I'd visited once before for a wedding and thought it less posh. We went up at the end of December; I was wearing the pink beanie that Joseph had seen everywhere at the start of our affair. There were electric-blue lights in the sky, and the whole family was present: my mother, Igor's, his grown-up children. I was less weepy but even sadder than the evening of *La traviata*. I could physically feel Joseph drawing back. Like a ball swept away by the wind, that you can only hope will somehow stop. Every metre further gutted me. My skin was grey: no matter what I did, the light had deserted my face. I was fretful walking along the seashore, and fretful walking along the rows of brick houses.

Facing the English coast, my feet in the sand, I struggled with the emotional injustice of it all. *Je suis la trace du désir de l'Autre*, as Lacan puts it. Yes, but what happens when the desire of the Other is denied, fragmented, buried alive? While mine has its faults too, certainly, but it's still full and stable and positive. What happens is that instead of flying into a rage, instead of saying: 'Go on then, you've pissed me off too much now, get out of my life,' the sort of person I am has an unwavering tendency to try to understand and adapt. To accept being dominated lightly. Calmly submissive. Morbidly patient. You can be a strong person and find yourself there all the same. The relationship becomes unbalanced – we can't stop it happening. We listen to the other's heart, and that's it.

*

Three years later, in October 2019, I'm looking through the photos of those winter days while stretched out on the king-size bed in the Chinagora hotel in Alfortville, a megalomaniac pagoda building, architecturally inspired by the Forbidden City, whose bedrooms look out on the river Marne. 'Ah, you're going to Chinagora!' a colleague said to me with a hint of envy as I was leaving the office with my backpack. Jérôme, who was dreading spending his week-end with his family, told me that one of his friends had got married there, ten years earlier. This hotel, now teetering on the brink of bankruptcy, was once the place to go for the south of Paris and the Val-de-Marne. Igor has gifted me two nights on my own there. He knows that I find the building impressive, that I want to film it along with the barges that go past, their headlamps on, along the blue, blue water of the morning. He'd rather know I'm there than in Ouessant.

Today Chinagora is a funny old decrepit hotel which puts me in a state of perfect anxiety. My floor seems to be quite full, but the others are terribly empty. The lacquered wood furniture in my room is disproportionately sized, and the breakfast is suspicious. Most notably, the scrambled eggs smell of special fried rice, which creates visual–olfactive dissonance and, consequently, distress. And then, on the seventh floor, more distress – the balcony overlooks the quays, the water, bridges, cranes and a stadium. A suicide spot with a message: *The growth of China terrified me.* I look down: it's very high up and there are big empty bins with their lids open beneath. Fear of jumping into them. I close the double doors: I'm doing well enough, at this point, to get these thoughts under control. I've even forgotten to bring the old strip of Xanax that I save for all my hotel stays and trips to towns of between 15,000 and 40,000 inhabitants (Tulle, Chartres).

Between sips from a bottle of Sanpellegrino, also over-sized, I scroll through the photos of that Christmas in Wimereux on my phone. I was doing badly, and in each photo I could tell you in what emotional direction I was being pulled when it was taken. I could tell you if it was a moment when I was holding back from sending him a message, a moment when I was waiting for a response, or a moment where I'd just received one and it was crap.

*

On Christmas Eve, towards the end of the day, as we hadn't got presents for our mothers, Igor and I had traipsed up and down the one commercial street. We were looking for cashmere scarves. He managed to find a red one that wasn't too bad. I touched the fabric with a distracted hand, 'Yes, it's soft,' while the other was gripping my phone in my pocket. I was waiting for it to vibrate. I knew that Joseph was writing something because I'd seen, a minute earlier, the three little dots bouncing on my iPhone screen. I was waiting, but the kids were pushing piles of polo shirts over in the shop, which stopped me from waiting properly. The shopkeeper was no longer smiling. Which is my criterion for starting to want the ground to swallow me up. I asked Igor to put a cartoon on for them. 'Please, they're making a scene, put *Trotro* on for them.' His phone in their hands, little cartoon donkey on the screen, my children squeezed up against each other in the fitting room.

*

Sitting on the lotus-flower carpet of Chinagora, I look at this photo of my kids. Even though we'd written our names in the sand together, I definitely spoiled this holiday with them, impatient and distracted as I was. I still had months left of living like that, out of step with everyone around me – still had months of further turmoil to come.

*

By the time we left the shop, the dots had stopped bouncing. The pixels were frozen. The screen was sorry: it couldn't invent words on his behalf. I felt like sitting down on the pavement and refusing to budge until a message arrived.

Later in the day, while I was busy not eating my portion of the Yule log (by that point, everyone was used to me not eating anything), a little red bubble appeared on Telegram. At first, I thought it was a trap: the encrypted messaging app has the same notification for a message received and for a new user on the platform. You think it's a declaration of love, and it turns out to be the Front National's lawyer (whose number I have for professional reasons). I turned my phone face down on the table: it couldn't be Joseph, who was spending the evening with his partner's ultra-Catholic family in Saint-Nazaire. Probably a French dinner of the coercive sort: 'We're moving to the lounge. Bring your glasses.' But I had to check, nonetheless. I slid my phone into the back pocket of my jeans and calmly headed to the toilet. Adultery's antechamber, now that most of us don't have a study like Alexandre Dumas *fils*. I typed the secret passcode into the app and read it. There was only one word: *Kisses*. He was sending me kisses. And? Sitting on the toilet lid, I waited a minute to see if the little dots would return.

They didn't. That was my evening ration, my daily bread, his Christmas wishes. *Wow, thanks.* I went back into the lounge to play with the children's new toy garage and their action figures. The grandmothers, full of seafood stew, were both happy as clams. It was irritating. I shook the Hulk. Feeling super negative, I made him complain about the price of petrol. What was he doing there anyway? He should be at the dermatologist's. Is there any present more annoying for parents than a plastic garage? What was the point of sending me that, rather than nothing at all?

The house in Wimereux was on a street running parallel to the seafront. Salty air coming in through the window. The bedroom was upstairs, with a nice parquet floor, and under the thick duvet, even though I was totally fine, thanks, I couldn't concentrate on the David Foster Wallace short stories I'd been given. The book was in my hands, great, but my eyes were wandering uncontrollably. I kept thinking about my stupid idea of the detente. I felt an urgent need to put an end to it. To send one of those definitive messages I'd regret forty-six minutes later, if it didn't get a response (aggression ignored withers so quickly). I held back until the evening, but on the train back to Paris I gave in. *You should know that you ruined my holiday. Your silences kept shattering the happiness of being with my family.* Joseph saw the message but didn't reply. I kept my head held high on the train platform, then on the Métro. I put Cat Stevens on through my headphones, 'Last Love Song', to remind myself that suffering is a shared state. And at dawn, when we could have been together somewhere, since my family had stayed down by the coast, I found a very long message in my inbox.

Joseph explained that it was idiotic to restart our relationship as if there hadn't been a break-up, and as if it wouldn't be painful if it happened again. So these silences, these absences, these scars of the break-up had to be cherished. Relying on this arsenal of silence was what would allow us to keep seeing each other. He understood that this ersatz romance didn't suit me at all: it was just enough to disrupt my life with Igor, while still far from rewarding in itself. But he thought that my way of seeing things was problematic, because obviously, if it all got too strong between us again, that would disrupt my life even more, and we'd fall back into the logic of escalation that would lead us *you know where, and this time I think it would be truly destructive.* So look, the name of the game, he said, was to see each other, to have sex, to do each other good, to make each other laugh, to enjoy each other's company. But not to have a mini relationship on the side, because we simply weren't capable of it.

The message seemed rather nicely done at first sight. The Josephian implacability, his uniquely recognizable intelligence. But time has passed and now all I see in it is a little masterpiece of gaslighting. Instead of saying, *I want you out of my life, but, since it's not happening, I'll make you hurt like hell instead*, Joseph affirms that my suffering is valuable and my demands are inconsiderate. Clearly, nothing exterior to himself exists. Things are conceived of in such a way to suit him. If in doubt, you just have to dissect his sentences to see the inherent contradictions. Problems emerge. Having sex and also letting silence prosper: that's just twisted. And in this message, there's that vague threat again. Destruction, devourment, division, decline – we never know what's lying in wait for us.

Don't destroy me pls.

According to a Seattle psychiatrist who's studied gas-lighting, it's made possible by a process of projection: when one person's unconscious fear is forcefully projected onto another. From the start of our relationship, Joseph pushed me to fear the catastrophe inherent in our bodies coming together. I would end up accepting this too-strong thing of his that he projected onto us, because when he'd tell me, a year later, that we have to be careful not to see each other too much because we incite such *monumental feelings* in each other, I'd nod my head wholeheartedly. *Yes, I know.* But, coming back from that holiday, I couldn't understand why I had to suddenly spend my days waiting for messages that were nothing more than the unrecognizable traces of their predecessors. However, I couldn't bring myself to break it off entirely, so I came up with a new strategy: a short period of abstinence. No-Joseph January.

*

I lasted slightly less than a day and a night. By spring 2017, I could feel the clock ticking – I started to come to terms with the fact that Joseph and I hadn't been on the same page for some time. But before that, there was the aborted attempt at No-Joseph January and an entire three months that he still needed in order to detach himself from me. A hellish period, in which he pushed all my buttons. Encouraged me to hold on to him: 'If we're still in love like this in two years, we'll have to make some decisions.' Then ignored me. On Telegram, which we'd been using daily, his status changed to *last seen within a week*. It felt ostentatious. My phone was generally sterile. Tapping on the screen did nothing. Neither did shaking it like maracas. Leaving it lying around and finding it again was the same. Nothing. The red bubbles didn't want to appear any more. Put like that, it sounds ridiculous. But the ergonomics of social media are designed to exacerbate our misery. The absence of those little coloured images put me in a state of withdrawal. At night I dreamed of notifications, and, just as the symptoms were setting in, I got one on the bus. *I've still got these feelings vibrating all through me.*

At the start of 2017, in the middle of this mess, we met at the bar of a brasserie. That evening, Joseph was looking at me tenderly, but his eyelids were heavy and his body hunched. His leather jacket formed an almost perfect arc linking the barstool to the counter. *Be careful. He's got something up his sleeve. Something serious to say.* After twenty minutes, I thought I could see it on the tip of his tongue. Joseph took a sip of beer. A second later, he said that his girlfriend might be pregnant. Might be. They'd accelerated the process because she was nearly forty. Nearly. 'I'd rather warn you now, it's surely going to happen.' Surely. Well. It was so concurrent with our own relationship that I couldn't tell who was pregnant: her, me or him. Say that again? He said it again. Anger rose inside me, anger that couldn't be vented in such a packed place. In that moment, my thoughts had, for once, seemed unspeakable to me. I had the horrible feeling of having been their launch pad. The driving force of their production unit. The desire I'd generated had been reinvested somewhere else. Like in a pump system. I felt robbed.

I was still busy checking my body was still intact, that nothing had fallen off, my arms and legs were still there, when Joseph felt obliged to add, 'I've always told you that my relationship was going very well.' At that, I felt the air being sucked from my throat. I wanted to shout at him that he was lying to me or lying to himself; that, if his relationship had escaped unscathed from what had happened between us, then it must be made of metal. *Shouldn't be too proud of a relationship made of metal, mate.* That's what I should have said. At that moment, never mind all the people in there, I should have got up, stamped on his foot hard enough to flatten it for good, and disappeared in a puff of smoke. My problem is that I was terrorized by the thought of my actions defining my character. The concern he was showing numbed me. He was standing in front of me; I wanted to warm my hands up in his hair.

I did nothing.

After that tragic beer, Joseph sent me an email. *I'm worried that you're angry. Or that you're not okay. Or that you are okay.* It's funny – that's the only thing he's ever been interested in: knowing whether I'm angry or annoyed with him. He couldn't care less about the rest.

*

In February 2017, Igor organized three nights in Seville for my birthday. This, despite me spending a good part of our life together telling him what a terrible mood European city breaks put me in. I'm suspicious of the plastic interiors of aeroplanes. Of the pilot's psychological state. Of the variations in the sound from the engines. I hate making so much effort for so little time, the exhaustiveness of the guides, the foreign public transport. Oh, and I'm very scared of flying. I suppose that's probably the main thing.

It's also a question of ego: I don't take well to always having to do what's expected of me. The choreography of it all: cabin baggage, going to see the Alcázar, eating tapas, having sex at least twice. I go by the Émile Littré dictionary, which defines a tourist as a traveller 'who only crosses foreign lands out of curiosity and idleness, who takes a kind of tour through the countries habitually visited by his compatriots'.

It's not just a question of taste, either. The city-break weekend provokes anxiety as well. From the moment the taxi pulls away from the house, I have the feeling of being a little flashing dot moving across a map. I'm submerged in depressing images, a lot like the ones I get when I have PMS. Three days before my period, I get the feeling, when I move, of being a perfectly unremarkable ant.

I had actually asked for Le Havre. I wanted to go back to the swimming pool designed by Jean Nouvel that, when I was pregnant, had felt like swimming in the clouds. A white flash. A transcendent experience for a few euros. But a man capable of hearing anything doesn't necessarily listen to everything. It was my birthday, but Igor had wanted to visit the south of Spain for a long time. 'It'll be great. You'll see.' It would be sunny, and we could even make a little detour to Granada (that wasn't true – he started, right there in front of me, looking at different travel options on his phone). 'Pack your bags!' We were leaving first thing in the morning, with a budget airline. Not from a nice, proper airport, but some prefabricated shed. *Does it have heating, or should I bring my gloves?* In the evening, we'd eat dinner on one Plaza de España or another. 'Without coats, in February, can you imagine?' On the table next to us, a couple loaded down with mardy teenagers and digital cameras. That defensive feeling you get when you're in a place that everyone else knows better than you.

In the taxi, on the outskirts of the city, Igor took some work calls while I discovered a Telegram message from Joseph declaring our love 'the living dead', but living nonetheless. *I love you too, I want you to know.* As Igor was absorbed in his conversation, I took the risk of opening the message next to him. But I was short of breath and didn't know how to breathe normally again: exhaling too sharply would risk giving myself away. The effect this message had on the weekend was disastrous. Catastrophic, in fact, because Igor and I were still very far from finding our way back to each other – the worst was happening – and because tourism doesn't put the father of my children in his best light. His oppressive-suggestions syndrome intensifies. 'Let me carry your bag.' No. 'Well then, give me your jumper.' No. He wears shorts, sandals and long socks. A blue Decathlon bag full of medications in his backpack, which he clips up over his chest. It's adorable if you love him. He can also quite easily go into a shop and then, as he leaves, unwittingly walk right back in the direction he came from.

During this trip, Igor wouldn't stop asking me if my heart beat only for him. The answer: absolutely not. I was as indifferent as a jellyfish and it made me sick. Like Sofya Yegorovna, lured away from her marriage by the manipulative Platonov in the Chekhov play, I could tell that it was down to a lack of resolve. 'Oh, what misfortune befalls us! Already days pass at a time without my husband even crossing my mind – nothing he says registers, his presence goes unnoticed. It's beginning to perturb me. What to do? *(She thinks.)* It's awful! We have been married so little time, and yet… And it's all down to him – to Platonov! I lack the strength, the resolve to resist that man!'

*

When I got back from Spain, Joseph told me he had a gift for me. In a secluded room at the office, we sat down at opposite ends of a big purple sofa. The same purple sofa on which I'd discovered, with him, the principle of female ejaculation. But that was in another life. Five months had passed since then.

The box was too big for the gift inside to be interesting. Never mind, I was touched – I tore it open and found a soft toy. A brown, white and yellow eagle. Neither big nor small. It had a solid backbone: something intended more to guard a shelf than to be cuddled in bed. It didn't provoke any particular feelings. Neither fear nor comfort. Bulging feet, the sort you expect to play music if you press on them. Unfolded wings that came down to its knees. A comic-book eagle, with the slightly shocked expression of a startled drunk. A pile of synthetic fibres of no apparent significance. I looked at Joseph, but he didn't look like he was going to give any explanation. Okay. He just pouted and said:

'Do you like it?'

'Of course, it's adorable.'

(When, two years later, still not understanding what that eagle was supposed to mean and sick of the sight of it, I stashed it away in one of my colleague's empty drawers, I stifled the same manic laugh I had held in on the purple sofa. In hindsight, it was spot on. The motionless wings, the lifeless predator, the illusion of flight. But also the way the soft toy exemplified Joseph's connection to others. You can never criticize a soft toy, its passive expectation of satisfaction. It's not even possible. You love it, even though it has nothing to offer but its existence.)

But in the moment, on the purple sofa, I was thirty-four years old and reliving the scene of my eighteenth birthday. I was at the Lycée Condorcet in Paris (good at maths, it's the moment to reveal). I lived in the Batignolles neighbourhood with my mother. Having grown up in Neuilly-sur-Seine, and not in the jungle at all, relationships from this period of my life stayed with me and I was in love with a tall blue-eyed blond boy living in the sixteenth arrondissement in Paris. Revision flashcards. His beautiful mouth, and the arch of his eyebrow. Antoine is the boy I lost my virginity to, one Saturday, early in the course of the evening, after a Techno Parade and before a McDonald's. After that, I was in love with him for six years, during which he'd come back to me from time to time. (Once, I was put on triple therapy because, in the same day, the condom we were using had split and I learned that a week earlier he'd been sucked off by a random girl in the toilets of a bar in Thailand. That sort of thing.)

Antoine lives in Brazil now. Unless he's changed drastically, he's as bad an emotional deal as Joseph. Both demand women's complete devotion. But at the time, I thought what we had was important. The day I came of age, he dropped by the birthday party at my house. He didn't know anyone, but he'd made the effort to come. His presence lit up my evening. Sitting on my mother's bed, I opened his present with trembling hands. I found a black Muji pencil case with, first-degree shock, four pens inside. Pink, turquoise, orange, purple. 'Oh, that's brilliant,' I said. 'It's a pencil case with pens inside.' And, 'That works out nicely, I didn't have an orange pen.' It still makes me laugh now.

On the sofa, Joseph was looking up at me.

'Aren't you going to give me a kiss?'

*

At that time, I could have filled an entire sketchbook with pictures of his body in different positions. Ten pages would be dedicated to leaving drinks – those were our moments, and I knew all his postures with a plastic cup in hand intimately. Even when I was in the middle of a conversation with someone else and he was in my blind spot, I could tell you how he was standing. Situate his centre of gravity. His frame moved me. In each place he occupied, my mind put a cardboard cutout. By the end of the evening, there were forty of them. I said goodbye to each one: it was an Easter Island of Josephs. A dear friend of mine likes to say about him, 'The guy's got no backbone – literally and figuratively. He's like spaghetti!' She's not wrong. But that's what makes his body interesting. The feeling that you could make letters of the alphabet out of him. No good at all in a fistfight, even though in his head he's fighting all the time.

In March, an intern's leaving party started at six o'clock in the big meeting room. The redundancy scheme was still clouding the atmosphere, so everyone drank to excess. By nine, the general mood was more like three o'clock in the morning. In the half-light, the stone staircase and wrought iron of the office building seemed to belong to a manor house. On the top floor, alone in the open-plan attic, Joseph took me by the waist. The solemn position I've already mentioned. His eyes were steady. His bottom lip was swollen like a grape. He put his hands on either side of my face and pulled on my skin like he was trying to get the circulation going. He gently squeezed my neck with one hand and pushed it backwards. Then he stopped these fetishistic manipulations and uttered the most intelligible things he'd ever said in our short relationship.

Sensing that I'd need to come back to this a hundred times, I kept a note on my phone. Here are the eleven sentences that constitute the break-up letter I never received. They all worked on me, in that they made me want to scream at the injustice, while keeping me quiet.

I wouldn't have been able to look after you
You would only have looked after me
You upset me all the time without realizing it
I wouldn't have been able to bear your violence
I realized that I'd miss my partner too much
I would have let you down
You would have kicked me out after three years
It's the first time someone's loved me without being
    tricked, it's weird
You're a pessimistic person, you don't see the good in
    anything
You've suffered more than me, I don't know why
I wouldn't get anything done if we were a couple

In the end, I understood that Joseph wanted to spend his life with a woman who's capable of letting things go. He reminds me of Jake Donaghue, the incredible character from that Iris Murdoch novel. A brilliant writer, utterly endearing; wandering about London and offering absolutely nothing to anybody. Or only when it's too late. He says he hates solitude, but he's scared of intimacy. The substance of his life is a private conversation with himself, which 'to turn into a dialogue would be equivalent to self-destruction'. Jake Donaghue passes over Anna, a girl he undoubtedly loves since he is 'greatly attached' to her, but whose problem is that she wants to take life intensely. Joseph, too, finds it ridiculous to live so emphatically and create dramas, when, as he once heard on a philosophy podcast, the human being is nothing more than an unreliable assemblage of physical particles, accumulated material surviving a certain amount of time in its environment, like clouds.

As for my 'violence', which those who love me would rather call 'lucidity', I have to admit that it's not the first time that someone's brought it up. It's undeniable that some of my friends wait to be in good shape before seeing me. They have to be, to hear me knock everything they say to the ground. Clip their wings before they can get going. 'You're telling yourself tales.' Shake them like a doll whose battery is running out. I am the great shatterer of illusions.

I've already said this, but I'll say it again: I'm very lucky to have had children with a man who can withstand all my criticisms: the blade hidden under the Breton headdress. Igor constantly asks me why I stay with him. I reply, 'Because you are my favourite little brioche. A giant baby.' But the truth is, the thing I couldn't do without is the affectionate comfort in the way we speak to each other. Anyone who heard us would find our exchanges brutal. Would think we were always fighting. But we're not. It's just that he and I aren't afraid of saying whatever's going through our heads. Nothing stagnates. Everything is transparent.

I often dream about my colleagues all arriving at the office one morning with bleached hair and acting like nothing is different. I cry out, 'People are so fake!' It's the beating heart of my anxiety, and transparency protects me. With Igor, our exchanges cut to the bone:

'Today I thought you were in love with me, but the dinner you've made tonight is crap, isn't it?'

'Yeah, it's terrible. Clearly I'm less in love than yesterday.'

'Ah, you should have said something. Is it because I've shaved?'

'Maybe. I like it better when I can see less of your face.'

I understand that there's something depressing about this type of conversation, but Igor and I like it. And the advantage of living with someone who doesn't do concealment is that you can contemplate him from every angle, like a Playmobil, and judge him on what you see. There are no hidden weapons, no morbid desires, no betrayals underway. No disguises, as with Mrs Doubtfire, my childhood nightmare. The man alone on the balcony is the same one who comes back into the lounge. You recognize him.

*

I'd always known that Joseph painted and collaged in his spare time. But I'd never seen any of his work, except for my name graffitied in blue on a canvas. In spring 2017, I realized he must be talented: a gallery offered to exhibit him, and that ended up driving him away from me again. He was going to quit his job to focus on his art. A new, unconstrained life opened up before him. Smoking cigarettes in his studio in the Marais and spattering colours over an easel. He went on holiday to Croatia, just when everything was kicking off and he had a million things to think about. And by the time he returned, he didn't love me any more.

I remember the lunch when I realized it. It was April 2017. There were four of us on the terrace of a pizzeria. He was sitting across from me. He was eating sloppily. To make the guy next to him laugh, he was doing unflattering impressions. I said to myself, *Oh, good, I think he's going to drool in front of me now.* But that *in front of me* no longer made any sense. Everything had changed. Joseph no longer looked at me after every sentence he spoke, to see what effect it had had. There was no longer an invisible thread pulling between us – just the smell of slightly burnt pizza dough. The journalists with us were no longer spectators in our little theatre of adultery, but Joseph's privileged conversation partners. It was over. On the way back, I slowed my pace. He eventually realized. He slowed down as well. The others were up ahead. I pushed him to talk to me. He said, 'Now I have this project to finish, I don't have time to love you any more.' And, 'Save your ass.'

Save your ass. God! Total panic. What a miserable conclusion. Definitive ugliness, ultimate vulgarity. Is that where we'd ended up? Had he really said that? Once I was sitting at my desk, I wrote those three words everywhere on my diary. How could he have said that? Fuck, who says that? I turned on my computer and searched the phrase in Google Books. I found an example in a James Ellroy book: 'I saved your wretched rich-girl ass. I killed the man who made you a whore. I gave you a home.' Yes, there you go: in general, we use this expression in the context of a reproach. *I saved your ass and look how you thank me.* I remember that afternoon I was so disturbed that I got a tomato soup from the office coffee machine. Laughing nervously. 'Ah, go on then, I'll try the soup.' Not a pretty sight.

It was while I was blowing on the pale-red liquid, standing in an empty hallway, that I thought of Eugene Onegin.

That evening, I rushed to find the Franco-Russian edition I'd studied in my final year of school. Like Joseph, Pushkin's character is a dandy who gets involved with a woman only to extricate himself a moment later. All his energy is spent maintaining his inconsistency.

> Your admirable qualities are lost on me –
> I'm quite unworthy of them.
> Believe me – my conscience vouches for it –
> marriage for us would be a torment.
> However much I loved you at the outset,
> once I got used to you, my love would fail. [...]
>
> We can't have back our dreams or youth, you know;
> I cannot give myself another soul.
> I love you with the love a brother feels –
> and perhaps more tenderly than that.
> Listen, and don't be angry at what I say.
> A young girl has a nimble imagination:
> she'll change her fancies more than once,
> just as a sapling has a change of leaves
> with each succeeding springtime.

Off you go, Tatiana. But don't be angry! As for me, what would he have to do for me to get angry?

Joseph's birthday came around and, despite everything, I still wanted to shower him with attention. I went entirely over the top, starting with the presents. My friends advised me to halve the number, and halve the intensity while I was at it. But in the morning, before he got to the office,

I left too many things on his desk anyway, starting with an envelope containing a note whose grandiloquence I'm ashamed of.

*

I have a pillow over my face when Igor enters our bedroom in the house on the Île d'Yeu. We're in the middle of the autumn half-term holidays in 2019. I didn't hear him coming up the stairs. Recently his footsteps have lowered in volume; his diet has worked. His belly is no longer an empire; it's now barely a kingdom. He's thin. Contrary to what he thinks, it ages him. But it doesn't matter, because there's been a development. Yesterday, back on the Plage des Vieilles, although I'd shown no intention whatsoever of doing so, he asked me to, please, absolutely not suck his right nipple. Five minutes later, while we were talking about something else, I caught it in my mouth. Igor jumped like a little goat, giggled like a schoolgirl and went to wash it off in the sea. I admired his stride down to the shore: he walks like a giant from a Claude Ponti book.

As he lay back down on his beach towel, he was still laughing. He asked me never to do that again, before adding that nothing had ever aroused him so much in his whole life. It wasn't over between us. Especially since Igor loves this island, which is the only piece of land that I'd sometimes like to be tied down to. 'My real life is here.' Mine too.

*

In May 2017, we had confirmation of his definite departure from the magazine. I say *we*; I was the only one who cared. Joseph set about emptying his drawers for an hour or two here and there, and started to only come in at random times. I developed certain strategies, some more blatant than others, to work out if he would be present at the general meeting or not. I hung about different corridors of the office. How would I manage to keep coming and going from this building? It seemed to have lost all purpose. It was as useless as a computer with no internet connection. I was seeing it anew and rediscovering its materiality, the lino and the water fountains.

One evening, since I missed him but could no longer tell him so, I threw an impromptu get-together in my office. It was eight o'clock. I ran out into the pouring rain to get some beers, with the goal of enticing people to hang around. When I got back, soaked through and out of breath, I sent an email to ten people to say that I didn't know where this crate I had before me had come from, but there it was, and that we might as well (why not?) drink them while we waited out the downpour. Of the ten, four arrived straight away. Not him. Twenty minutes went by. I thought to myself, *Well done, caught in your own trap – now you have to talk about work with these people you don't care about.* He opened the door. I feigned relaxation. We were opening the bottles and started talking about French rap. A topic I have nothing to contribute to. As always when I see him talking with other people, I was struck by his method: presenting grumbling defences of nebulous theories while simultaneously caricaturing them so as to distance himself.

111

After a while, the conversation was going in circles. The four others got up. He said, 'Hang on, I'll come with you.' I said, 'Oh, I'm going to stay for a bit. I need to tidy up.' He didn't bat an eyelid. I watched him put on his coat and leave without turning around.

The light from the ceiling spotlights was orange. One of them was crackling. It was still raining. The ten computers around me made me feel outnumbered – they were many, and united. I put the empty bottles in a bin. I fell onto my chair, rolled back and forth in it, and waited for him to come back. In my heart, I felt the same way a ten-year-old girl does when she's just seen her old best friend cross the playground arm in arm with a new chosen one. That kind of solitude. The feeling that something has irremediably changed in the way the other person perceives you. The feeling of having lost the power to seduce, the way you lose your youth.

That night, I dreamed I was having dinner with the family of an internationally renowned pianist, whose son actually did want to marry me when we were at nursery together. In the dream, I was his fiancée. We were talking about guestlists and caterers. In the morning, while showering, I tried to work out the meaning of the dream. Then, as I was getting dressed, it hit me: the pianist's son has the same name as him. Duh. The following night, I was transported to the streets of Venice. Next to the Grand Canal, I caressed the hands of a bad actor with a mop of thick hair. The same as his. It's amazing what the nocturnal brain can do to keep the affair going, without losing face.

*

At home, everything was sad. I couldn't quite put Igor back on his husband pedestal. I actually preferred his body by far, but I had forgotten all about that. I was blinded by the ease and urgency that Joseph had injected into my sex life. Particularly the horny-teenager vocabulary. The words *dick*, *cock*, *cum*, *ass*, which made my stomach ache with pleasure. The empty meeting rooms, so much more exciting than the marital bed. My imagination had been colonized. One Sunday, while we were having lunch in a restaurant with our children, Igor and I discussed our sexual problems. In English, I told him that he needed to give me some time to come back to him. 'Stop it – anyone would think you'd been kidnapped by Genghis Khan!' We had a good laugh at that one. I added that he could also try saying more dirty, or even sordid, things to me in bed. At the time, he joked about this New York scene: the tribulations of the fifty-something intellectual with round glasses and his unsatisfied younger partner. But it's cruel to ask someone to change their sexual personality, which is like being yourself but after a thousand calculations. Later, I realized that he'd resent me for a long time for having suggested that.

The saddest thing was that during that time, I no longer liked the things that I'd always loved about him. His attention focused entirely on his children. His mother-hen side. His way of saying *fishy-fish* for fish, *chicky-chick* for chicken, and of suddenly calling us all *sweetie* made me want to throw up. While we were walking through the forest and I heard him telling the boys about the coronation of Napoleon, I was exasperated. I walked ahead. He caught up with me. I said, 'I don't think we're going to make it.' My B-movie saying of the time. As if we only had three francs left in the shoebox to get us through the winter. I was sick of the history lessons that left me sidelined and silent. Sick of being with a man who preferred the company of children to adults because they devote more attention to him. Sick of living with a friend, a brother, an all-powerful mother.

That day in May, after many more *we're-not-going-to-make-its* launched like rockets from my chaise-longue, Igor told me to stop. That was enough. I was hurting him. Could I look him in the eyes for one moment? He was hurt. He couldn't take my selfishness any more. Having a family came with certain responsibilities. You couldn't just send people packing like that. Yes, no, you couldn't submit to the natural cycles of falling in and out of love like you did before. Or less so, anyway. You held your horses. You looked before you leaped. You didn't just set sail at the first sigh of a lover. You used your brain. You had to look in front of you, at what you'd built, and, since it was good, you should want to take care of it. Being part of a couple was like building a cathedral. It was the sum of all the days all together that made sense. There was nothing worthwhile and no glory in anything else. Yes, of course it was sad that 'trying out a thousand men' was no longer on the agenda for my life. But when was I going to snap out of it – or leave? When was I going to at least put a sock in it? I was wielding too large a threat. He wanted his no-clothes fight (throwing the boys naked onto the bed before their bath) and to hear them sleeping. Every night. Not every other night. He had tears in his eyes.

Shortly after that conversation, Igor started to have intrusive thoughts about our two boys. That is, he started to be afraid of hurting them when I wasn't around. He couldn't bear the sight of a rope, a knife, a saw or a hammer. I've had that, too, at the end of my maternity leave, when they were tiny. I know how it feels and I reassured him: 'No, you're not going mad, and you're not a murderer either. It's nothing. Just anxiety coming out through these thoughts.' That led him to go back to therapy and me to wonder what I had done by not leaving him to go through his grief alone. What abyss had my presence covered? Would it open back up again if we separated? Left on his own, Igor would FaceTime the boys every evening to say goodnight. It would be impossible to refuse, and it would take hours. He would call back an hour later to see them asleep. He wouldn't be able to get to sleep without a body to hold on to. So he'd call me back again. And he'd start eating more again. He'd feel abandoned on a Sunday, in the swimming pool changing rooms: *I waited for you at locker 61, like an idiot.* Then, no more news. He'd console himself by seeing his long-time flirtation, a member of parliament whom I rather like. To try to make me laugh, on the phone, he'd describe his future wife: 'The next one will be petite and shy, and I'll be able to tuck her away in a drawer.' It would make my chest feel tight to hear it. But the worst thing would be that I'd also have to live without his comforting welcome at night: when I get into bed, his arms open instinctively: 'Come here, you're cold.' Without him, there would be no one to put vitamins in my mouth. No more strange withdrawals on my bank account, no more English breakfasts. Extravagance would

115

be gone with Igor, leaving me in my Breton silence, which is no good unless there's someone else to put an end to it.

The father of my children came out of his therapy sessions with one major idea: he hadn't allowed himself to feel angry enough with me. He was furious with me for cheating on him. He hated me meticulously. There you have it: when my break-up with Joseph was actually completed, Igor finally got angry.

*

Walking past your therapist in the street requires composure. Particularly when you haven't been to see her in a long time. Resist the urge to stop and ask how she's doing. A therapist is an individual whose consubstantial mystery must be preserved. Give her a faint smile, letting her know that everything is going very well in your life now, she can rest easy. But don't force it too much. That would be a sign of instability, a guarantee that she'll say to herself, *Yes, there was still work to be done with that one.*

As we live on the same street, Madame A. and I bump into each other quite regularly. I clock her from a distance and prepare a little Chaplinesque smile. Only once, when we'd passed her, did I turn to Igor and murmur: 'That was my therapist.'

'Where?'

'In the red coat behind us. Be discreet, but it's her.'

'She's short, isn't she?'

On Joseph's last day at work, Madame A., who isn't short and whose hand I hadn't shaken in years, received an

S.O.S. via text. Her door was already ajar when I reached her floor – I could see her hair through the gap as she waited just inside. She opened it wide. I greeted her without meeting her eye. I went into the hallway. A screen hid her blue-walled living room. Five steps further, I automatically turned left into her office. A small rectangular room with a view of the Eiffel Tower, with fancy notebooks and books on the subconscious scattered about. In psychoanalysis we call this the frame: a place that's at once familiar and partially untapped, where you can spend years alongside objects that never enter the restricted visual pathways of a classic session, when one is recumbent on a sofa (it's probably comparable to Louis XIV's chambers for the Versailles servant who guards them every day).

It was five o'clock, but already getting dark. I sat opposite her, slightly ashamed. The first time she had helped me, the situation had been objectively complicated. I had extended a grieving family. It was important, almost a public service, to help us find our respective positions in this new situation. I was arriving this time with the newborn wail that romantic rejection provokes. Arms had let me go. Biting the armchair would have done me good. But I described my symptoms instead. I was fairly sure a black liquid had flooded my insides. And my head had been switched off. After a break-up, certain areas of the brain that have been stimulated by all the romantic excitement go further than just going back to sleep. They turn on you.

Madame A. waited for me to calm down. The first thing she said, which did me a lot of good, was that it was important to have tested, once in your life, the limits of your own willpower. We can't always do what we want. I had the proof, and I couldn't cope with it. Well, at least I'd gained something: maturity. She added that it was time for me to accept Joseph's refusal to go any further, and to let the heartbreak happen. In time, I would feel the jubilation of freedom. At the end of our session, she suggested I read Freud's *Mourning and Melancholia* and start psychoanalysis after the summer.

Coming out of that first session, I had clear objectives. I slowed my rhythm of getting in touch with Joseph. *Don't suggest lunch before September. Don't reply within the hour to the emails that you're not going to receive.* In the bath, before falling asleep, I replayed the key arguments for falling out of love with him on a loop. Often, I did it in the form of a little quiz. Could I name a single person that Joseph cared for on a daily basis? Other than his own interests, what motives did he act upon? Had he ever been aggrieved by an injustice? Had I ever seen him take any risks? What risks? Was it tolerable to spend time with someone who always throws a double threat back in your face: intrusion and abandonment? So then why did I love him so much?

I bought Freud's *Mourning and Melancholia*. Reading it on the Métro, I learned that it's natural to resist the disappearance of a loved one at first. You can't simply erase an attachment. Can't order your psyche to just get over the lost object and reinvent itself. With non-pathological grief, 'proof of reality' will always triumph in the end, but it requires spending a huge amount of time and energy. Every memory and hope has to be taken back and worked through before the libido can finally break away from the object.

A good student, I made a list of my memories and hopes with Joseph, and I tried to undo them manually. That's all I did, actually. Relive, file away. Admit that it was behind me. *Come on, libido, let go.* And when I dog-eared the pages of Freud's book, I thought of Igor and his wife and Joseph and me in turn. I couldn't stop myself from drawing a parallel between what I'd put Igor through with Joseph, and what he'd done to me by bringing me into his life too quickly. I found what we'd done to each other to be of the same nature, just part of a life lived to the full. We are monsters who love each other.

In Igor's mother's cluttered apartment, there are two photos from his wedding that don't make me feel anything because they look like they're from the Fifties. The clothes, the hairstyles, it's all from another era. I never dare to look at them too closely when I'm there because I don't want her to think I'm jealous. But I see them from afar and they make me smile. Igor has a round little baby face. On the other hand, not too long ago, at the end of the double lounge, near the glass table that injured one of my sons when we'd gone over for tea once, my mother-in-law added a photo that does hurt me. Igor and his wife are sitting in a restaurant, on opposite sides of a table that doesn't manage to separate them, holding hands across it. They're celebrating their daughter's graduation – they're so proud of her (as they should be, there's no child more accomplished). In this photo, Igor is giving her the tender look he usually reserves for babies when they've just been born and belong to him. A look that seems exhausted by the infinite tenderness it conveys. I no longer dare go near this photo because, the few times I have, I've felt like leaving the house. This image tells me that she is his wife. Which is, by the way, what he still calls her.

*

In July 2017, the moment arrives: Joseph leaves the magazine. On the evening of his last day, I received an email in which he declared that the past year had been unforgettable: he had loved me enormously and I would stay with him. He hoped that I would find peace again soon. As he was very bad at maintaining friendships, he couldn't be sure that it would happen, but he also promised he would try to keep me in his life a little bit. The email ended with a *see you later.*

My abandonment. With all the means of communication this century affords us, he wasn't sure he'd manage to *keep me in his life a little bit.* I was devastated. The first month of his absence, I heard nothing from him. The second month, still nothing. I thought he must be pissed off at me for something. I demanded an explanation and immediately felt like vomiting. I couldn't take any more. We had been going over the same material for a year now – it was as absurd as repeating the same word over and over again, but still, we met up in the Jardin des Tuileries. The Jardin du Luxembourg was the first pin on our Google Maps of Tenderness; the Jardin des Tuileries was the last.

This time, our chairs weren't turned towards each other. We were both facing in the same direction. I'd sprayed myself with the perfume that always sways him and put on a ridiculous backless thing. Joseph told me that the things he wanted to say were *getting stuck in his throat*. Okay. What things?

Firstly, he was pissed off that I'd tried to psychoanalyse him and then use that to criticize him, even if I was sometimes quite right (I was momentarily flattered), when I no longer had any right to do so. Secondly, he accused me of making sarcastic comments about his relationship. Of taking pleasure in their passing difficulties. One day, I'd made fun of them because they were homebodies. I had said one thing and thought another. It turned into a row. He used the words *gleeful nastiness*. What, what, what? That day, I finally understood that there was an underlying bad blood between us. The problem was right in front of me. This boy I loved hoarded the microscopic contentious details that floated through our conversations. Then he used them to break us up. I discovered that we never both experienced the same conversation. That nothing could ever be certain and that, in reality, he had been mining my words for this very moment. Is that why I replayed each of our exchanges a hundred times in my head as if they each contained an inherent trauma?

By the end of my second can of Diet Coke, Joseph had added that he wasn't in love with me any more and that with all the work he was going to have – three new commissions had just arrived in his inbox – he wouldn't have any time for friendship. A ship's anchor was wedged in my oesophagus. I hardened my face so it wouldn't betray any emotion. By some miracle I managed not to cry. I know Joseph can't tolerate it. My sadness envelops him and makes him want to shout, *I'm not your torturer.* I replied that he had taken his time to admit to me that we weren't on the same page any more. That he'd kept me on the line, letting me convulse in front of him without saying anything.

'It's true, I could see you were suffering and needed me to look after you, but as your former lover it wasn't my place. I might well have kept loving you, but I never changed my mind about ending things.'

In the end, he said it was a shame that we'd had another pretty unpleasant encounter, instead of the good time we're also capable of. At the entrance to the Métro, I smiled as I said goodbye. Like him a year earlier, in front of a Métro station in south Paris. A part of me was relieved. For six months, I'd been fooling myself, shaking a plank of wood to try to get it to wake up.

*

The world is divided into those who leave you and those who stick around. The summer of 2017 came to an end, and the school year started up again in our office building, now empty of him. September. I thought about him 145 minutes per day. Two to five times per hour. He was the first thing I thought of in the morning. When I walked down the street, I imagined him watching me walk down the street. When I passed the places where we'd stopped, even for a second, to kiss or whatever, I was assaulted by a series of flashbacks. When, after my shower, I found myself naked in front of the mirror, when the lighting was good and I thought I looked nice, I had to stop myself taking a picture to send him. I resisted, but grief was progressing too slowly. Everything was made more difficult by the fact that my workplace was saturated with memories and that he could come by unannounced to say hello to other people. Which he did from time to time. Without coming to see me. I'd always find out later.

I wasn't asking for more than one real-life interaction per month. Lunch, a beer. As for the rest, no more than one text every two weeks. I wrote to him when the need proved impossible to stifle. Then some mundane thing would start to look, in my head, like an excellent pretext. I fabricated opportunities. I'd send him a photo of a general meeting, the result of a vote, an in-depth analysis of an office rumour. I was his union correspondent, for want of being anything else. Essentially, I was offering him unlimited availability. A senile war widow, opening all the windows in the house so the ghost of her husband can come back in. Most of the time, Joseph left the conversation hanging. He never did me the honour of closing it in any reassuring way. As October came around and the days got shorter, some evenings I realized that night had fallen without me thinking of him all day. But that still counted as thinking about him.

Now, Joseph no longer occupied my conscious thoughts, but what was perhaps worse, he took up residence deep down inside me. He became a fixed point of my preconscious. Like a pre-holiday shopping trip to be done that niggles at the back of your mind. But very gently: a finger tapping a remote control. And then, something happened that derailed my convalescence.

In November 2017, Joseph, who had just sold a series of canvases soberly christened *Red Squares*, let me know that he was going to buy a studio just a kilometre from where I lived. No need to worry. Without admitting to himself what he was doing, he'd walked the route between the studio and my apartment: it was a safe enough distance, we wouldn't be bumping into each other every Sunday. I thought, *Okay, but now it's going to be on my mind at the weekends, too.* That was true, but it wasn't the worst part. The worst part was that, from that moment on, I never again knew if I was going to the square near his workplace simply because I liked it or because I was increasing my chances of bumping into him. Before he decided he just had to invest in my neighbourhood, I loved that square. I went there all the time. So why did I now feel guilty each time I headed down there? My decision of where to go had been sullied forever. And it bothers me to admit this, but I have noticed that I never set foot in the other square any more, which I also like very much, but is in the exact opposite direction from Joseph's place.

*

I reconnected with Igor in fits and starts. I have a sunny lunchtime in the main square in Arras in mind. He's finishing off an article over a steak, his head is half hidden behind his laptop, but I find him handsome and rugged, and I like what he's writing. We order some mulled wine, and the belfry watches over us. Or on holiday, near the Château de Chambord. At a Chinese buffet (grills, woks, sushi), we have our most hilarious moment as a family to date. I haven't gone for the standard €18 all-you-can-eat option like Igor and his children have. This has aroused the suspicion of a waiter and a waitress, who are keeping a close eye on me to make sure I'm not dipping into any of the off-limits dishes. We can all see them hiding behind the plants, watching my every move. Clearly, I look like the kind of girl who can't be trusted not to hijack a bottomless menu. I share a conspiratorial smile with Igor as I twirl my fork in my hand, wondering how far I can take it. Then I spear a forbidden dumpling. They spring from their hiding place, pounce on me and snatch my plate away. I raise my hands in surrender as the others fall about laughing.

During this time, Joseph disappeared into his success. The only incident of note was a sole email argument, naturally due to his radio silence. I got annoyed. He got annoyed back. I had to understand that he didn't have written conversations with anyone. He insisted: *anyone*. The written word was sneaky and false. It was all style and turns of phrase. He felt obliged to spend hours thinking about each sentence. For example: right there, in the preceding sentence, what was he going to do about the unpleasant connotations of the word 'obliged'? He didn't want to take it out. There you go, it took him time and concentration, and he didn't have any of that to spare.

Sure, but if the story didn't end there, it's because his great rejection eased up. At the beginning of the year 2018, perhaps because of a lack of inspiration or because things weren't going so well with his partner, he started hanging around the office again. Maybe once a week, he could be spotted out on the crappy boulangerie's terrace. The one from our early days. And here was the real problem: he started to show little signs of desire in front of me again. He let up completely after months of denial. I'd come up to say hello to him. He'd get up. Smoke coming from his ears. Cheeks turning as red as the Napoleonic Code. Mouth exiting stage right. Strange noises coming from his throat.

A few weeks later, he upped the ante: declarations of resurgent desire started to arrive. At the end of one day, in the property reporter's empty office (he's never there, that guy), Joseph told me that he couldn't change his sexual focus: 'I've tried, but I always come back to you.' He was still filling, a year after our *break-up*, lengthy Word documents with sexual scenarios starring me. He also thought that we had some magic between us – that our erotic fantasies were in sync. That wasn't true, for my part. By that point, my sex life was back to normal. But I suggested that we could kiss.

'No. It's forbidden.'

'Forbidden by who, Joseph?'

'By the Bible, for a start.'

Unfortunately, all it took were those three sexually charged words for me to partly fall back into it. That evening, I found myself back on the autopilot that kicks in when passion is first sparked. Floating above my family. Wanting to be on my own so I can properly think about *that*. Replying 'Good idea' to everything. Subsequently, as his confessions – arousing, physical – became more frequent, I managed to keep them at more of a distance, but never succeeded in fending them off entirely. It went like this: I'd see Joseph buzzing around me; I'd suggest we do something about all the sexual tension; he'd refuse, making a weird little pelvic movement; and I'd go about my life more or less preoccupied for the next few days. One evening, we were in the street. Since he wouldn't stop staring at the ground, I wound up asking him, 'What do you actually want, Joseph? You want us to go back to a hotel? Right now? Tell me, so we can be done with this!' Like he'd received a punch to the gut, he bent double with desire. He put his hands flat on the wall in front of us: 'I do want that to happen again.' Then: 'I want to be inside you, but it's so risky... It's not the right time at all.' Why risky? 'Because we're not going to be able to stop.'

We spent several months in this middle ground that reminds me of my driving: one foot constantly on the brake, accelerating too hard with the other. If I was in a good mood and not telling him off for anything, we only had to spend half an hour together for the merry-go-round to start up again. He would sit and admire me 'like a Turner painting'. He'd smile when I made a clever point. He'd launch into a funny monologue about modernity. He'd say: 'We're one step away from falling in love with each other again.' Then, with misty eyes, he'd let me know that his insides were getting warm and his dick was getting hard: 'I can't even look at you without wanting to be inside you.' He was far more explicit and adventurous when he knew he'd be far away the next day – on holiday or at an exhibition abroad somewhere. Faced with imminent departure, he had twice dragged me into the foyer of a building. His hands suddenly everywhere and between my thighs. His swollen lip pulsing at the level of my nose. A spike of desire might also happen when he was faced with a transparent blouse, a pair of tights, or a new haircut. I'd had it cut it very short, it was as stupid as that, but he was overcome with emotion. Stock still, red-faced and overheating in the middle of a shopping street; people stopping to watch us like it was a scene from a romcom.

'You know, since I told you I wasn't in love with you any more in the Jardin des Tuileries, I've fallen in love with you again a hundred times. Or, to put it another way, I've never really been sure I wasn't.'

So, at the start of 2018, I found myself in a bit of a sticky, possibly forbidden, situation, built on the foundation of his desire and my stubbornness. How, when it came down to it, could we sustain this? Having considered it at length, I think the problem was that I gave all the information I received from Joseph the same weight. The magnetism and the repulsion. My decoding system was scrambled. I no longer knew which was the truth. One cancelled out the other. Not knowing was holding me back. On Joseph's part, it was a question of maintaining some internal balance. In *The Work of the Negative*, André Green – him again – perfectly describes people like Joseph, who behave according to a principle of non-displeasure (that's what guides their lives). However, they also have to be wary of pleasure. Resist their drives. Suppress the temptations that crash around inside them. *It's forbidden.*

In Woody Allen's *Match Point*, Chris Wilton, the tennis coach, is considerably fitter than my former lover. To be fair, I don't exactly have Scarlett Johansson's body myself.

Mine looks more like it's been passed through an industrial machine: I'm a big, flat rectangle. But these differences aside, the tennis coach is, like Joseph, tormented by a carnal passion that threatens the course of his life. What he feels for Nola (Scarlett) is violent and involuntary. The girl becomes a sort of demon for him. He ends up shooting her at point-blank range. I'd rather take Joseph, who only ever shot me in his head and actually cared about me a lot, though he tried not to show it. I've been asked about it, but I've never detected any conscious malice in him. I believed him when he told me he was trying to protect me from our unhappiness.

*

Now a father of twins, Joseph tied himself in knots to never utter their names in front of me. Then one day, without warning, he brought them with him to the office. The news reached me too late, and I didn't have time to escape. I found myself in the middle of a group of old journalists, having to gush over their slightly questionable resemblance. One of them, clearly teething, took my biro and gnawed on it.

And by dint of sharing the same neighbourhood, I eventually wound up bumping into them all together. It was a Saturday afternoon; they were leaving a restaurant. I was on the pavement opposite, but I saw them straight away. I was badly dressed – an old sweater that's only fit for the countryside. An overgrown fringe. In no shape to be faced with their beautiful unity. I fixed my gaze on the horizon and walked faster, but Joseph flagged me down. I crossed the road, smiling. After a pause, his partner started talking to me about the GPs in the area. I couldn't find a single intelligent thing to say. Without realizing it, I managed to derail the conversation from general practice to pelvic-floor rehabilitation. She gave me a strange look, but I'd started down the path and I couldn't stop. I heard myself repeating the words *electrostimulation*, *vaginal probe* and *perineum contractions*. Joseph couldn't believe what he was hearing. In a high-pitched voice, I babbled two final idiotic things about episiotomy and dashed off without saying goodbye.

I came home to an empty apartment. Igor was in the countryside with the boys. I made a coffee and lay down on the sofa to rest a little, while on the inside I was being stabbed by a thousand tiny blades. That encounter had reminded me that a partner existed, occupied her place and had been chosen over me. She watched him eat and wash. She could, upon waking, raise her arm in the air and let it fall on Joseph. Watch him stand up to choose a book, while I only knew his back from watching him walk away. To calm my nerves, I tried to draw up a list of my good qualities, but I could only see myself through a hostile lens. I was the girl he didn't want.

After two hours spent on the sofa, I was a husk. Huddled in the corner, I looked at the apartment walls and thought about how they would outlive me a thousand times over. I was so insignificant that even the partitions would outlast me. Fear returned. Fear of giving up, of drowning in my own banality. I was like a Richard Yates character when they're forced to admit they're not a hero. I would just have to keep pedalling, dispassionately. The years would pass, my teeth and hair fall out. I would become set in my ways.

The possibility of rebellion, or even changing direction, would steadily diminish.

At some point, the evening hubbub started to drift up from the street, and I thought maybe things weren't so bad after all. In the end, under the pink marble, all our lives are equal.

So that's where I was in spring 2018: still capable of being paralysed by sadness. At the magazine, two friends helped me stay the course of my dignity. 'Remind me why I shouldn't message him?' They did. In the meeting room, they listened to me talk about him again and again. One was reassuring: 'He's just protecting himself, but he loves you really.' The other stoked my anger, asked questions designed to make me realize the necessity of leaving him and came up with some interesting metaphors: 'He's a big pointy knife twisting inside you, and you don't know whether or not he's going to let you grab him by the handle.' But it was all well and good being wise – as soon as her back was turned, I behaved like a child. *I sent an email.* She didn't scold me. *Time is the only way out of this, but hearing the truth will reinforce your willpower to wait it out.* One day, after sending one message too many, I thought, *What if you decided not to be a child, and stop throwing him the ball?* So I walked around, for several days, weeks even, with a metaphorical ball in my arms. Him: *Are you angry?* Me: *No. I've just changed our rules of engagement.*

Joseph didn't want to hear about change. My presence in his head was his business. It was now quite pleasant for him, and he didn't understand that it could be different for me. *Put your hand between your legs and think of me as you fall asleep.* When he talked about us, he invoked the notion of wu wei, the Taoist concept of letting the cosmic order run its course. He referred to Laozi: 'We can't change our relationship, *it is what it is.*' I replied, without conviction, with Walter Benjamin: 'That things are "status quo" is the catastrophe.'

I wasn't joking. I wanted us done.

TAKING FLIGHT

Rue Charles-François Dupuis, near the Place de la République, bears the name of an astronomer who died in 1809, a child prodigy with a talent for geometry: he could calculate the height of a tower with the naked eye. It was on the corner of this street, whose length he could have easily estimated, in a bougie café with tartan blankets draped over the chairs, that I met a comedian whose star was on the rise: if, when I met him in September 2019, he was still performing his show to a tiny room in Paris, a few months later he'd sell out provincial concert halls. That day, we were supposed to be writing his talk for a conference my magazine was organizing. He was late. I saw him arrive from afar and, since there's nothing more embarrassing than watching someone walk up to you, gazed pensively into the distance. Louis's head was hidden under a Levi's hoodie, which was a compulsive habit of his. From a distance, he didn't look like much: he's not particularly tall, not particularly well built, not particularly anything. But up close, he had a very lovely face and salt-and-pepper hair. I said to myself: *He should be a model, the ones they always have coming out of the water dripping wet.*

Perhaps because I couldn't shake this image, of him covered in drops of water, we didn't talk about work at all that morning. We went from café to café, talking about our personal lives. He's a bit younger than me. Doesn't have kids. Lives nocturnally. Works in his kitchen. Only wears black, white and grey. Watches lots of American TV series; I'm not familiar with any of them. I told him about my life: Igor, my children, my supervisor who has no boundaries between work and his private life, the disappearance of print media. He rolled cigarettes for us both and asked a ton of questions. As I answered them, he nodded his head so hard he must have strained his neck. He would liven it up, then send the conversation in a different direction. We thought it all through together. Our trains of thought merged. It was as if he were trying to make us deliver the best account of our lives. I've never experienced that with anyone else. There was a unique nuance in the way we spoke to each other. It reminded me a little of late-night teenage conversations. I'd actually never experienced these myself, as I'm incapable of relaxing on the phone, but I saw one of my friends do it once when we were younger. Lying on her bed. Lighting and relighting the same cigarette butt over and over.

So, every time one door closes, another one opens, and at some point Louis, who had been a maths teacher until three years before, told me how comedy had changed his life. We discussed Erving Goffman, the American sociologist who studied social interaction and whose theories were sometimes unwittingly stand-up material. Think of his description of the unease we feel at the idea of moving away from the person sitting next to us on the Métro after the carriage has emptied out. As I felt I could confide in him, I talked to him about my passion for video art, much ridiculed and impossible to reconcile with motherhood.

'But really, my kids are older now. I'm just making excuses.'

Louis asked me if my partner managed to find time for himself. I replied:

'Well, yes, of course. Since we got together, he's written several books and led a campaign to clean up our local streets. Every Saturday, at the crack of dawn, he'd get up and go round the arrondissement, taking pictures of piss-trails on the pavements, and then post them on social media. That took some audacity, but it was very successful.'

I added that I'd done a very good job during this time, spending entire days traipsing around different freezing squares.

Louis didn't laugh. He'd finished rolling his cigarette and was looking at me. I'd already realized by this point that this boy had a very different worldview to mine. Essentially, he lived on a diet of feminism the way I live on a diet of psychoanalysis. He was militant and thought in terms of action and change. And so, what had to happen happened. Louis abruptly set his coffee cup down on the table. The conversational bliss was shattered. The pseudo-erotic river scene crumbled. The cars queuing next to us came back into the frame. He exclaimed, 'Well, you have to fight back!' I couldn't let a creative and intellectual imbalance become the norm in my relationship. I had to fight for myself – and for other women: 'You have to find a way to create space for yourself.' I felt, in that moment, all the lacunae of my apolitical upbringing in Hauts-de-Seine. And I felt the urgent need to make a video – something allegorical, absurd and vaguely artistic – to mark the end of my relationship with Joseph.

When we said goodbye, it was next to my electric bike with its fluorescent yellow child's seat. Where I apparently like to attract the people I find most brilliant. As I was unlocking my bike, I said, 'You know, thanks to you, I'm going to close a chapter of my life.' Then: 'I'm sorry to unload all that on you like that, I'm aware that it's intense.'

Completely unfazed, Louis replied that he was ready to help me with my video and he was sure he'd been nothing but a 'link in the chain'. That last part was true.

*

Among the protagonists of this final act, let's put Madame A. at the top of the bill. A little while before I met Louis, she had gently hinted at the idea that we were going, in the near future, to start, perhaps, to think, just a little bit, about ending my sessions. I had been seeing her twice a week for two and a half years at that point, since Joseph had left the magazine; I loved her as much as it is possible to love someone from a horizontal position, and I wasn't expecting this at all. I let a silence pass and then moved on to something else entirely, not yet ready to talk about our separation:

'So, in this weird dream I had last night, there was a Chinese woman who was actually me disguised as my mother. Like in our last meeting, it's the same theme of disguise and confused identities.'

My psychoanalyst has never used the word, but I know all about the Freudian concept of sublimation. The idea is that the sexual drive is redirected through creative exploration. The libido is channelled into acts of higher social prestige, and so the object is possessed, in a different way. It's a possible and rather desirable outcome of psychoanalysis. And it just so happened that, two days before I met Louis and threw myself into this video project, my analyst had shaken me in an unprecedented way. How many times can you listen to the same person complain about the same thing?

'He says yes to the desire but no to the rest, which in his head equals destruction. You're not going to risk losing Igor for someone who tells you no, are you? You can flirt, but it's a no to the rest. You have to decide it for yourself, in your own head, too: it's over, and it's a no.'

At the end of the session, she gave me a high five. That always sparks a need in me to please.

When crediting the muses for my plan, we must finally mention the great actress, star of the Eighties, who I met for a magazine piece on love letters. It was in the same café as Louis, a week earlier. I'd thought of her because as a student I'd been extremely affected by a book containing dozens of letters she'd written to the love of her life, a director, who was somewhat older than her. This love story reminded me of mine with Igor, even though theirs had a very different character. Her partner was gigantic and Alsatian. Mine is short and Russian. Their relationship, indeed their whole life, was maintained to a high standard, while ours accepts

139

its primitiveness. Between them, love remained courtly and immaculate: highly sophisticated language, intellectual films, separate apartments and steadfast formal address. A love story à la Sartre and de Beauvoir, which had survived similar affairs. Igor yells my name down the aisles of the supermarket and is known to make jibes like 'Ugly!' and 'Looking rough!' when he passes me in the hallway at home. During a recent argument, when I refused to go and hash it out in our bedroom and drove the point home by sitting on the kitchen floor and kicking him, he dragged me through the apartment by my legs like a caveman in a comic strip.

The day of my meeting with the actress, I was totally starstruck. I'd rewatched all her films. I turned up very early, my stomach in knots. After a long wait, I saw her enter the café, dressed all in black and not as tall as I'd imagined. She immediately asked to move tables to somewhere less noisy. I picked up my things and went ahead of her, like a lady's maid. Right at the back, in an isolated booth, she was satisfied. For two hours we talked about her elegant love letters. Then, my oversharing filter being poorly calibrated in professional contexts, too, I told her about the entanglement I'd taken so long to get over. I wheeled out the image of the abandoned dog.

She understood entirely.

'Yes, of course, it's like a dog left by the side of the road, it's the body that doesn't understand. It's crazy, being a girl. The body takes time to go back to how it was before. Men don't realize: women always give more. He should have taken gradual steps backwards. Leaving someone from one day to the next, the way he did you, that's called an abuse of power! You need to get it out of your system. Make some kind of gesture; the fact that there hasn't been any is why you're still talking about it. It needs to be wrapped up, closed off, cauterized. You need to find the words or the action that will allow you to leave it behind. There's power in finding your autonomy as a human being who's been left. Your dignity. Even if you only write one sentence, *I am writing to inform you...*, you must write it and send it to him first class.'

I found all this interesting, but I couldn't stop myself laughing internally at the thought of Joseph's nervous face as he opens the envelope. *I am writing to inform you that I am pissed off with you forever.* I had laughter rising in my throat, but I tried to contain it because the actress was serious and intelligent, and because she was giving me further advice.

'You ought to swear at him when you see him in the corridor. He penetrated you psychologically, and then he left again. It's like an enemy occupation. He got his claws into you. Find the strength to be angry about it! In the end, you're the one who will leave him behind.'

This was by far the best conversation I'd ever had on the subject. I would have liked it to last for hours, but I had work to do, and we turned the conversation back to her. Luckily, after five black teas and an interesting lesson in Lamaze breathing techniques (particularly humiliating in public but I didn't dare say no), she came back to my problem of her own accord.

'You should try, for at least a few seconds a day, to look at things from the height of the heavens. Get on a plane, mentally. From high up, you can see the people who make you suffer more clearly. Change the path you're on, make something out of it – it's the substance of your life, it's what feeds art. It all has to ferment and petrify before it can come out. I think this is your moment. What you've been through, it's a good thing, because you know the states we can get ourselves into. But most of all, it's up to you to turn it into something you can learn from. Tell yourself you've treated yourself to this, the way you might treat yourself to a meal at La Tour d'Argent.'

*

Madame A.; the admired actress; Louis: these three encounters contributed to the hatching of my bizarre and liberating plan. But we mustn't underestimate the involvement of Joseph himself. Not unironically, he was the first person to give me the idea to transcend our affair through art. It was just after the falling-out-of-love lunch at the pizzeria. He said, 'By the way, you're not going to go and make some extravagant video out of all this, are you? I won't stop you, I like what you do, but I won't hide the fact that I'd rather you didn't.' When he put the idea forward, just after having dropped the *save your ass* on me, I had no idea what he was talking about. I was hurting so much that it was impossible to think about anything else. And anyway, my only plan then was to get him back. Since then, I've read somewhere that the best position to capture a subject is simultaneously interior and exterior to it. That must be true: it's the ideal position. When the mind is still stimulated by what has happened, but there's been a detachment. From there, it's possible to reclaim the facts.

It happened eventually, with Joseph: a definitive distance grew between us throughout the autumn of 2018. The circumstances helped – now his star was on the rise, he spent most of his time travelling. He never came to the office any more. To not know what he was up to, all I had to do was not read culture magazines, which is quite easy really. Absence led to forgetting. After a long period with no contact, Joseph occupied only a tiny, cold plot in my mental landscape. Even the idea of a friendship disappeared. In the end, I just felt a great weariness towards his general lack of generosity. *In every aspect of my life, I'm never the one to take the initiative.* I ended up tiring of his way of only replying to one message out of three.

And then, in November 2018, there was the final aggravation. I had gone to the Alps, to report on the story of a cyclist killed by a hunter who had mistaken him for a wild boar. That evening, when I arrived at the station in Bourg-Saint-Maurice, it was already nine o'clock. I was alone at the foot of the mountains, a curtain of snow falling in front of me. In the sky, currents of fog swirled like steam rising from a saucepan. The hotel I'd booked was three kilometres away. There was no sign of life on the esplanade by the station, just the flapping of a plastic bag. I googled the numbers of local taxis, put on my best little voice to convince them to come and pick me up, but they were all finished for the night. My trainers were soaked. I headed to the café over the road, which still had its lights on and seemed like it might have rooms available.

The owner's daughter, who couldn't have cared less about my predicament, told me they'd all been requisitioned by the council to house refugees. And that was that. She was testing microphones for karaoke night. I thought to myself, *Stop feeling sorry for yourself and just sing*. We performed several Elton John songs together. After the third, the girl started to warm up to me. By the fifth, we were friends. That's how I learned the importance that karaoke can have in a person's life. She had got to know her boyfriend on a karaoke website that connects people through singing. On her laptop, she showed me their rendition of Francis Cabrel's 'Je l'aime à mourir' (a perfect duet between Bourg-Saint-Maurice and Paris). After three months spent like that, he'd decided he wanted to be more than the right side of her screen. He'd come to Bourg-Saint-Maurice to sing in her ear instead. It's not always easy: he does long hours in a spare-parts factory, and it's colder here than in Paris. But it works. At midnight, she finally offered to drive me to my hotel and pick me up in the morning so I wouldn't miss the bus to the ski resort where my interview was to take place. (The offer was so generous that it made me suspicious: later on, I double-booked it with a taxi reservation the hotel made for me, and I fell asleep, feeling anxious that the two cars would arrive at the same time.)

So, drunk on alcohol and Elton John's 'Sacrifice', I arrived just after midnight at this two-star establishment in Bourg-Saint-Maurice. The corridor floor was covered in duckboard matting, which reminded me of the worst parts of ski school.

The bedroom was a bit sad, too, the ubiquity of brown (bed linen, floor, walls, furniture, curtains) giving the room a claustrophobic feel. I turned off the main light. I didn't take a shower, just put my trackies on and slid between the scratchy sheets. I turned on my phone torch, wedged it under my chin and opened *Serotonin*, the latest Michel Houellebecq novel. I've always read his books with great curiosity, but since I've known Joseph, it's become almost joyous. The pessimistic intelligence of his characters always reminds me of him. And this time, too, it didn't miss: Florent-Claude Labrouste, the hero of *Serotonin*, talks in exactly the same way. The same way of complaining about everything. Of not getting too involved. The same nebulous theories. I smiled when I read the passage where the narrator strictly advises against real communication in relationships. For him, open conversation leads to reciprocal understanding, which in turn inevitably leads to disaster. Communication between men and women doesn't produce love, but division and hatred. To guarantee a lasting love, he recommends 'an affectionate, formless, semi-linguistic babbling'. To speak to each other the way you would speak to your dog.

The next day, after eating breakfast in front of a blinking Christmas tree, its lights alternating on and off every three seconds, I went and stood in the hotel car park. The girl from the karaoke skidded through the snow at eight o'clock on the dot: no Parisian I know would have done that. In the car, we sang some more. Once I was on the bus, to distract myself from thinking about the bends in the road, I messaged Joseph to tell him that Florent-Claude spoke, the way he often did, too, about women 'in the pre-feminist sense of the word'. Feeling soft, I suggested we get a coffee once I was back. He didn't reply. By the evening, I was on the train home and getting annoyed. I sent him a scathing email, like in the old days, with a subject line whose idiocy now paralyses me: *One-way relationship*. This time, he spoke up: *Stop acting like you don't know how this works. You know full well that I only use my phone to make calls and that I'm slammed with work. I'm sick of getting worked up over these things. Obviously we'll get coffee. I'm always around the office. No need to set a date.*

*

That was the moment I reached the summit of self-hatred. It had to be the last time I put myself in this position. I would never beg him for anything again. In fact, this latest little dispute, combined with the lack of oxygen at altitude, finally woke me up. It took a second after having taken two years. I was struck by the utter drivel of our conversations and our games. The neuroticism of our relationship was suddenly clear to me. Every interaction between us ended badly for me. It was over. Because, when life subjects you to the same pain again and again, discovering it's your own fault is unbearable. You have to keep moving. Get out of there, like Daimler in Frédéric Berthet's book, a private detective whose business isn't going well and who's unlucky in love: 'I've decided to stop taking on new cases, and clear off. [...] There's a moment in life when everything leads back to the previous case. And that moment is terrifying. Then soothing. So soothing you could fall asleep in the snow. If you can agree that hell is repetition, then you can understand that I'll make myself scarce before entering into that hell of repetitions. The damned are condemned to eternal torment, the living to repeated misfortunes.'

Repeated misfortune. After my trip to the Alps, Joseph made a surprise visit to the office. A colleague and I had lunch with him. He told us all about his world tour of art galleries. Then, given the cases of sexual harassment going on in the art world, we talked about feminism. Joseph contested the very principle of the movement. He argued that men are the real victims of our times. He said that he was harassed every day – on the Métro, in the street – by psychotic men. Every day, yes, definitely. Said that you had to think about the percentage of the male population in prison. That the wage gap was bullshit. How much was I paid? Well, there you go – that was more than he had been! And we mustn't forget who had gone down the mines and off to war in previous centuries. By the end of lunch, I was exasperated. He turned to me. 'Are you pissed off?' I replied, 'No.' I wasn't. I knew it was just his sense of self-preservation talking.

Repeated misfortune. A month later, in December 2018, I bumped into him on Place de la Madeleine. He was wearing an orange beanie (he stole my bright beanie look). He was smoking outside the Kenzo boutique, shopping bags at his feet. I thought he must be rich now, and about how, only a few streets away, the Seine separated us from the Assemblée nationale. It was a straight line from here. I didn't yet know what I would do there a year later. It was nice chatting with him. His collages were selling very well in Asia. Still all squares? No, he'd moved on to diamonds now and that was going even better. By the way, he had news of Yann and Sophie from the crêperie in Rennes. They'd bought one of his canvases for €3,000. It was their wedding present. We decided that meant we weren't allowed to mock them any more. Then, after a complicit smile, we decided we could just a little more.

As Joseph was in the mood to joke around, he switched to his sarcastic ribbing mode. Was I still enjoying journalism, i.e. lying to people to get interviews? Was I still making my little films with no narration? Did I realize that no one could name a single figurehead of this contemporary pseudo-art? A few playful comebacks about diamonds came to mind, as well as the excellently named video artist Pipilotti Rist, but I just laughed. When we said goodbye, pleased with this drama-free conversation, Joseph took me in his arms and said *oh là là* twice. 'Oh là là. Oh là là.' Waiting, as usual, for me to duly note his desire and suggest we do something about it. But, for the first time, it didn't carry any weight at all. It was what it was: an urge obstructed somewhere. A biological reaction that I could play with, like a cat – or not. An isolated fact. While love is something else entirely. It's a matter of resolve.

*

In the year 2019, things were completely restored with Igor: we became once again a couple with ten years under their belt who go through ups and downs. Distant, close, distant. Zero calls per day, then ten. Not at all keen on making love, then a bit more keen, then suddenly very keen, but it's already been a month since anything happened, etc. And then, bit by bit, what had recently seemed romantic started to look hellish again. Long car journeys together. Being squashed under all his weight at night. Grabbing his legs in the swimming pool while he's trying to practise his breaststroke.

Recently, Igor has also grasped the concept of weekends away in France. We've just spent one near Solesmes Abbey, a thousand years old and three hours north of Paris. We arrived on Friday afternoon at the reception of the Grand Hotel. The manager, educated at the finest hospitality school, had a firmly polite smile as she advised us to reserve a table for dinner right away. Igor said no. Still on his diet, he had brought quinoa in his clipped-up rucksack. That evening, we were in our pyjamas by eight o'clock. He prepared our dinner in his square Tupperwares. We were so happy to be together that we called the grandmothers to ask them if they could look after the kids for an extra day. The next day, we went to buy warm socks in Sablé, where the last few cultural revolutions have passed the clothes shops by entirely. I tried on a fake-leather raincoat and a purple bra.

Our fireworks are few and far between. Once, I took the children to the Île d'Yeu, when Igor wasn't supposed to be coming with us. As we were getting off the boat, I spotted a grey-haired man ululating on the pier. 'I've already done the shopping, you just have to hop on your bikes!'

On the wild coast, under a drizzling rain, the children up ahead, Igor and I talked about my affair again.

'We got through it in the end, that whole thing. You didn't leave me.'

'You know full well the power your body has over me. I'll never find better.'

'The truth is you put up with me.'

'Yes, I put up with you. You're a force of nature. You fight against sadness, you give life texture. You do weird things, sure. Like cheating on me, filming the trees in Corrèze, being with me in the first place: it's all part of it.'

The same evening, singing 'La Madelon' to himself, he made his special salad for everyone: rice, tomatoes, and barbecue-flavour crisps crumbled over the top. But he himself only ate three apples, two sardines and a pear. That's one of the things threatening us these days. His successful diet. Igor has no belly any more – it disappeared three weeks ago. A related problem that I'll have to keep an eye on: he's now trying to make me eat all the food he won't let himself touch. For some time, he's been smearing every dish I eat with Roquefort. Roquefort omelette, Roquefort pasta, Roquefort broccoli. I'm sure he's thought about feeding me Roquefort in my sleep.

Over the next few years, we'll have to see if Igor and I can live together without making each other suffer. If I let myself go in my forties, it's likely that the Anne Pingeot syndrome will subside in the end. And if I become a sort of grandmother figure to his daughter's children, it's possible that this family's force of attraction will have become so strong that I won't be able to pull away. So perhaps marriage will be for the best.

From here on out, we'll be confronted by the thousands of problems our living together poses: the teacups and yoghurt pots he strews around the apartment as if he'll one

day need to find his way back, the politics books he piles
up in the hallway, our lack of common interests (the Third
Republic for him, André Green for me), our social incom-
patibility with each other's friends. Which means that we
often find it's just the four of us. Me, him, the children, like
we're on a little boat. And the fact that once we're outside
the apartment, our lives are completely separate. I couldn't
tell you if that will be our undoing or our salvation.

*

One day in November 2019, I was walking through the
Jardin des Tuileries with my friend Charlotte. We were
talking about her older son, who is overly attached to her,
when, as we walked into the Jeu de Paume gallery, I stopped
mid-sentence. I was struck by an artwork taking up an entire
wall. It was by the entrance to an entire exhibition. I recognized the geometric shapes. I had to sit down; I was seeing
stars. It was a mix of *lítost* (if he was so famous, I didn't
deserve him any more), of despair at having so clearly lost
the thread of his life, and a new grief to go through: grief
for the pleasure that the possibility of associating myself
with his success would have given me. Once I was on my
feet again, my instinct was to get closer to see if there was
something of me in that canvas, a trace, some influence. Or
even a message. I stepped over the barrier protecting the
artwork. Perhaps that yellow mark, in the lower left corner?
An attendant asked me to step back. I obeyed, steadying
myself on her arm, which took her by surprise.

Charlotte hadn't grasped the gravity of the situation.

'Ah, it's Joseph's exhibition! Do you want to go?'

'No, I'd rather not.'

I told her to go on without me. I'd wait for her outside. I sat down near the spot where he had told me, more than two years earlier, that he wasn't in love with me any more. I thought that I now belonged to his past and that as such, even if I couldn't give him a shock like the one he'd just given me, I'd undoubtedly cross his mind, several times a year, without ever knowing it. It would happen whenever he stayed in a Kyriad hotel or filled a Breton bowl with hot water. When watching a movie featuring a small-nosed brunette, I imagine. Beyond that, it's hard to say. It seems unfair that our names aren't locked away somewhere, sealed together for eternity in the heavens. I searched, in literature, for short, life-changing affairs, and could only think of André Breton's *Nadja*. At the end of the book, he says to the woman who has taken Nadja's place: 'It's perfect how you have hidden her from me.' Would other women take my place, in Joseph's memory? How many, and when? Would he think that it was perfect? And who would know about us, in a hundred years, when I'm buried in Brittany, where the gravel is wet and the salt eats us away? I want a mausoleum with a watertight roof and Italian music. I want to be buried with a big pillow and the men who have loved me. My final thought was that my affair with Joseph had been beautiful. His artwork was beautiful, too.

Charlotte arrived, smiling.

'Feeling better?'

'Yes.'

*

The act took place a year after our encounter outside Kenzo and a few days after the shock of the artwork in the Jeu de Paume. The affair was over, but I still felt, as the admired actress had predicted, the need to make a gesture. To begin with, I thought of doing it on 12 December 2019, to coincide with the date of our break-up three years prior, but in the end I brought it forward, out of fear of dying. An irrational fear, but not completely delirious, since the preceding days had brought more than their fair share of dangers. There had been the Ikea wardrobe that had fallen on my head. Then there had been the taxi driver with a red shovel on the passenger seat who also, making what was an already very serious situation worse, wouldn't let me open the window. I couldn't shake the idea that he was going to diffuse a poisonous gas through the speakers.

I meet Louis in front of the statue of Jean-Baptiste Colbert, Louis XIV's minister and proponent of the 'Code noir' that presided over slavery. There's a light morning drizzle falling on the Quai d'Orsay. The Seine is choppy, its surface wrinkled all over. On my right shoulder I'm carrying Igor's blue Decathlon bag. I take out a tripod that I set up at the end of the Concorde bridge, on the pavement opposite the Assemblée nationale. I set my phone up on it and ask Louis to wait for me as long as it takes. He's shivering from the cold, but he pulls up his hoodie and says, 'Okay, but be as quick as you can.' At the entrance to the Assemblée nationale, I show my press pass and say very loudly to the security guy, who absolutely could not care less, that I'm here to cover the bill on audio-visual reform. He peers inside my bag, then at me, with an interrogative look. I say, 'It's a gift for my godson, he's arriving from London this evening.' He shrugs.

I've studied the building's floorplan on the internet. Once I'm inside the Assemblée, I cross the four-columned hall at high speed. I almost knock over Jean-François Copé, who's actually not an MP any more. That flusters me for a second. I take one of the staircases leading up to the press platforms of the assembly room. Once I'm up there, I cross the guard room much more carefully, since this is the space reserved for parliamentary journalists. I adopt the countenance of a parliamentary journalist. Hands by my sides, a deeply humble expression on my face. On the right, I recognize the window that gives access to the roof of the decorative pediment designed by Bernard Poyet. This façade has the allure of a Greek temple and resembles the one opposite, of La Madeleine. The interior of the triangle that dominates it originally depicted Napoleon offering the flags captured at Austerlitz to the legislative body. But the design has been changed twice in the course of two centuries. Smiling, I think back to the emperor's journey from Elba to Paris in March 1815, dubbed 'The Flight of the Eagle'. Walks with Igor have given me a specialist education in Napoleon.

I open the window. It's slippery, definitely very danger-ous, but less so than taking an aeroplane. I put my hands flat on the damp slate and begin my ascent on all fours. Without looking down. At the top, I grab the pole of the French flag to stop myself from slipping. I have vertigo: it's like when I was a little girl, on the six-metre diving board in the swimming pool that I forced myself to climb up ten times. I signal to Louis, who starts the camera. Passers-by have grouped around him. They've got their phones out, thinking they're about to see him livestream a republican suicide on social media (Louis must have explained to them that it was actually performance art about a break-up, because then they asked if I was Sophie Calle).

With one hand, I hold on to the flag very tight, and with the other I take the white, brown and yellow stuffed eagle out of the bag. The psychoanalyst François Roustang has this expression I really like, which describes the moment when the cure has finally worked: it's when you've *worn out meaning enough to return in the end to the thing*. For a love affair, I imagine that you could put it like this: it's when *you're worn out by it all enough to throw the thing away*. Although I'm offering him an exceptional and symbolic taking-off point, the eagle is as impassive as ever. Louis signals to me that I can go ahead. I stroke the bird's head and tell it, 'Whatever happens, it's not your fault. We do what we can.' Then I throw it as hard as I can. It follows a nice bell curve trajectory. It falls without unfolding its wings. Straight down. Completely rigid. Still with that slightly shocked look, like it's just been told off. Arse first. On the ground, it rolls down the pediment steps and ends its journey in a puddle, on its right side. The cops are already down there, waiting for me. Several weapons are trained on me. A squad surrounds Louis, who pleads for mercy.

Alone on the roof, I murmur, 'That went well. Bravo.'

ACKNOWLEDGEMENTS

Thanks to Catherine Nabokov, my first reader and editor, my ally and my agent.

Karina Hocine and Charlotte von Essen, Charlotte Hellman, Gregory Messina, Audrey and Renée.

TRANSLATOR'S ACKNOWLEDGEMENTS

The translator would like to thank Ruth Ahmedzai Kemp and Bryan Karetnyk for their invaluable guidance on the Russian literature in this text, and Martha Stevns for her expertise on psychoanalysis.

THE PEIRENE SUBSCRIPTION

Since 2011, Peirene Press has run a subscription service which has brought a world of translated literature to thousands of readers. We seek out great stories and original writing from across the globe, and work with the best translators to bring these books into English – before sending each one to our subscribers, six to eight weeks ahead of publication. All of our novellas are beautifully designed collectible paperback editions, printed in the UK using sustainable materials.

Join our reading community today and subscribe to receive three translated novellas a year, as well as invitations to events and launch parties and discounts on all our titles. We also offer a gift subscription, so you can share your literary discoveries with friends and family.

A one-year subscription costs £38, including UK shipping. International postage costs apply.

www.peirenepress.com/subscribe

'The foreign literature specialist'

The Sunday Times

'A class act'

The Guardian

PEIRENE | STEVNS

TRANSLATION PRIZE

The Peirene Stevns Translation Prize was launched in 2018 to support up-and-coming translators.

Open to all translators without a published novel, this prize looks to reward great translation and to offer new ways of entry into the world of professional translation.

The winner receives a commission to translate a text selected by Peirene Press, the opportunity to spend two months at a retreat in the Pyrenees and a dedicated one-on-one mentorship throughout the translation process.

The Peirene Stevns Prize focuses on a different language each year and opens to submissions from October to January.

With thanks to Martha Stevns, without whom this prize would not be possible.